Taken

By Selena Kitt

Chapter One

"What's the matter, Lizzie?" Sarah squeezed my shoulders, her hair brushing my cheek as she leaned over to peek at the papers strewn over the desk.

"My hundredth hang-up tonight!" I rolled my eyes toward the phone. "They finish half the stupid survey, and *then* they decide it's too long and hang up."

"Don't sweat it, hon." She reached across me and gathered my completed surveys. "Don just went home and left me in charge. Let's knock off ten minutes early."

I plopped my pencils into a cup and stood, stretching, my shirt pulling up out of my jeans. Sarah poked the eraser end of a pencil at my navel as she passed by, and I laughed, following her toward the office.

"David... Tina... Chad... Stacy... Lynn!" Sarah trailed her hand across each cubicle as we walked by and heads popped up one by one. "Turn 'em in folks! Time to go home."

I followed her into the office, heading past her toward the small fridge.

"Throw me one." She sat down, kicking off her heels and putting her bare feet up on Don's desk.

When I touched a can of Mountain Dew to the sole of her foot, she squealed.

"Nice polish. Can I borrow it?" I tossed the can to her and she studied her toes.

"Sure."

"I'm outta here." Stacy slapped her surveys on the desk. "Eight good ones."

I stuck my tongue out at her overachieving back as she walked away and Sarah grinned. Chad and Lynn left together, arm in arm, without one survey between the two of them completed.

"What a waste." Sarah sorted surveys on the desk. "Teenage hormones! What were they doing—calling *each other*?" Tina left her surveys and was gone without a word. David was still putting things together in his cubicle.

"He's waiting to be alone with you." I watched him through the two-way glass.

"Not gonna happen." Sarah snorted. "Besides, work relationships are bad news. The male-female power struggle is tough enough without adding that to it, right?"

I shrugged. "He's cute."

Sarah laughed. "How easily you forget that you're attached at the hip to a certain stud who picks you up here every night...or is there trouble in paradise?"

"No, but..." I grumbled. "He's not picking me up tonight. He's going out with 'the guys.'"

"Aww—so you have to spend a night all alone?" She mock-pouted. "Welcome to my life."

"Here ya go, Sarah." David gave me a steady look as he came in the office. He was clearly wishing I wasn't around. She took the surveys and sorted them onto the desk, acknowledging him less than she had anyone else tonight. "So what are you girls up to on a Friday night?"

"Not much." I might as well not have even opened my mouth. He was all about Sarah.

"How about you?" David nudged her. "I'm meeting some friends at Industry tonight—want to come?"

I watched her, half-smiling. Did he really believe the woman known around the office as The Ice Princess was going to agree to go to some dance club with him last minute?

I watched his jaw work as he waited. I felt bad for him, knowing Sarah wouldn't say yes, even though I knew she wanted to—some part of her did, anyway. She wouldn't admit it to me, of course. Not out loud.

I'd told her, one slow Saturday we spent hanging out in the office, how I'd go for David in a heartbeat if I weren't seeing Tim. I'd never seen Sarah turn so cold—and that was saying something. I knew immediately, in spite of her objections, she had a thing for him. She told me right away to drop it—she insisted she didn't want to talk about it.

So, of course, I teased her about it constantly. That was the way things were between me and Sarah. And, really, I wasn't kidding about David. Yeah, he was older, practically old, but he was *hot.* If Sarah dated him, I cajoled, I could at least live vicariously. She tolerated my teasing, rebuffed me with sarcasm. That was Sarah.

She sat in silence for a moment, glancing at me and seeing the light in my eyes. "Actually, Lizzie and I are having a girls' night."

"That so?" David looked over at me. I neither confirmed nor denied—I just smiled and looked away. "Well, sounds like fun. See you two later." He went out of the office to get his jacket.

"He's not a bad guy." I shut the door and lowered my voice. "Besides...have you seen his basket?"

"His what?" She wrinkled her nose.

"His basket. His… you know…" I cupped the crotch of my jeans as if there were a bulge there.

"Oh Jesus, Lizzie, is that all you think about?" Sarah laughed. "There's more to life than sex. He's a thirty-five-year-old telemarketer, sweetie…"

I raised my eyebrows. "So are you."

"I'm a telemarketing *supervisor*." She fished her purse out from under the desk and slipped her shoes on. "Besides, he's not my type."

"You keep saying that." I rolled my eyes. "Methinks the lady doth protest a lot."

"Too much." Sarah smirked. "Methinks the lady doth protest too much."

"Exactly."

"Hey." She stood, slinging her purse over her shoulder and looking at me, considering. "How would you like to actually do a girls' night? I can cook. We can rent a chick flick. You can borrow that nail polish. What do you say?"

I hesitated and then shrugged. "Why not? I don't have anything else to do."

"Gee, I'm glad I'm a last resort."

We both grinned.

* * * *

It was pouring outside, and by the time we'd rented *Unfaithful*, it had developed into a full-fledged summer storm. We were both shivering and wet, and Sarah turned on the heater in her car. I pressed my hands against the vents in an attempt to warm them.

"Feels like summer is officially over." Sarah's teeth chattered as she pulled into the parking lot of her apartment complex.

"Sarah, your lips are blue."

"Yours are purple." Her eyes lingered on my mouth for a moment and then she met my eyes and smiled. "Ready to run for it?" It was raining so hard the windshield was a waterfall.

"On three."

We counted together, opening the doors and running toward her apartment. Sarah stopped to slip off her heels, hopping as she did it, and that put her ahead of me. She beat me to the door and we both stood there shivering as she fumbled with her keys. The warmth of the apartment felt good, and I set the movie on the table near the door.

"Come on." Sarah unbuttoned her wet blouse, heading toward bathroom. "Let's get out of these and put them in the dryer." I followed, hesitating only a moment before pulling off my wet *Coldplay* t-shirt. She threw her blouse in the dryer, turning to grab my shirt.

"Jeans too." She turned her back to me. "Will you unzip me?" I unzipped her skirt and she slid it off and threw it in. I unbuttoned my jeans, rocking them down my hips. They were wet and came off hard. I toed off my shoes and threw my socks and jeans in with the rest of the clothes. She turned it on and smiled brightly at me. There were curly, wet strands of blonde hair stuck to her cheeks. "They'll be toasty warm by the time we're done with dinner. How's pasta sound?"

"Great." I followed her out of the bathroom.

Sarah started a fire in the living room in the gas fireplace near the sofa, and she made me sit there with a glass of wine. I wasn't much of a drinker—hadn't even gone out to celebrate my drinking-age birthday the year before. Sarah, I figured, was thirty-something—I wasn't completely sure of this, but it was my best guesstimate.

"This will warm you up in no time." She headed back to the kitchen.

I watched her go and realized I was sitting there in a bra and panties. It was very warm in her apartment, and Sarah didn't seem uncomfortable with our state of undress as she puttered around the kitchen, preparing dinner. I could watch if I turned sideways on the couch and put my legs up, so I did.

"Can I help?"

She shook her damp, blonde curls. "Nope. I'm fine."

"So...what's the deal with you and David?" I couldn't fathom her rejection of him. "You can't deny he's a total hottie."

"He is, isn't he?" She smiled, stirring the pasta. "Well, for one, he's divorced. Hard to trust a guy who made a go of it and failed, you know?"

Ouch. Harsh. But that was Sarah—no one else we worked with could stand her. I was the only one who could tolerate her caustic remarks, even when they were directed at me.

"And, well...he works for me." Sarah shrugged, putting something together in another pot. "And you know how Don harps about work relationships."

"What about Chad and Lynn?" I snorted, knowing Don, our "big boss," looked the other way a lot. "They're permanently lip-locked and they work together."

"Oh, them!" She waved a dismissing hand over the pasta pot as she blew on it, keeping it from bubbling over. "They're on the same level, you know? It's just not comparable."

I sipped at my wine, which was almost gone and Sarah came to refill it.

"Hey!" I laughed. The fire was warming me outside, and the wine was warming me inside. I felt flushed. "You trying to get me drunk?"

"Might do you some good." She tipped the bottle a little further, filling my glass almost to the top. I just rolled my eyes, watching her refill her own glass and set the wine on the counter.

"I don't need to get drunk," I mumbled into my glass.

"No?" Sarah licked wine off her lips and turned to stir the pasta. The sauce pot next to it had come to a slow-motion boil, splattering red sauce on the white glass surface of the stove. "I think you need something like it."

"Sure you don't need my help?" I offered as she slid a lid onto the sauce pot and shimmied it around for a moment before setting it on a back burner, reaching into the cupboard above her head to bring down a colander without even looking. I thought she was brave to cook in so little clothing.

"I got it," she insisted, dipping a fork into the noodles and picking one carefully off the tines. "And don't change the subject."

"I'm not." So what if I was? Sarah tossed a noodle at her kitchen wall and it stuck there, making a strange pattern that reminded me briefly of the Arby's logo before slowly peeling away. She caught the strand and tossed it into the sink. "Was the wall hungry?"

She smiled as she picked up the pot and moved toward the sink. "That's how my father taught me. The spaghetti's done if you throw it against the wall and it sticks."

"I'd hate to be around when you cook a pot roast."

I loved when I could surprise a laugh out of her that way, when it wasn't just a polite thing, but a genuine response. There was something so bright about her in those moments it made my chest ache. I watched as she plated our food, putting down silverware on cloth napkins, which had been carefully folded in a basket on the counter, before calling me to the table.

"Come on, let's eat."

The meal was warm and filling, although I didn't pay much attention to it. Sarah peppered me with questions.

"So what's after college?"

I sighed, twirling spaghetti with my fork like it was all I could think about. "I don't know."

"Have you and Tim talked about it?"

"Me and Tim..." I gulped some more wine, my eyes watering. Everyone always assumed we were an item, like we were one thing, one mind, one entity. Not that we weren't. We'd been together so long, sometimes even I believed it. And sometimes it drove me crazy. "Yeah, I guess. A little."

"First comes college, then comes marriage, then comes Lizzie pushing a—" Sarah nudged me under the table with her bare knee and I jumped.

"Don't say it!" I stuck out my tongue. "You sound like my mother."

"Life reduced to a nursery rhyme..." She shook her head, still smiling.

I watched her sip her wine, tuck her hair behind her ear, cut her spaghetti into pieces as if she were preparing it for a child. I wanted to say something, to break things open between us somehow, but I didn't know the words.

As if she understood, she tipped her head at me and asked, "Isn't that the usual order of things?"

"Who says I want to be usual?" My eyes didn't move from hers.

"Now we're talking..." A smile crept over her face, a smile I'd never seen before, something devious, exciting, her eyes lighting up with it. "And here I thought you were just gonna be another good sorority girl turned real Orange County housewife...."

"Well..." I dropped my eyes to my plate, feeling something heavy in my chest. "I probably am..."

"Not that there's anything wrong with that."

"Ha." I snorted. "You don't believe that for a minute."

"Life changes you." Sarah ate spaghetti with a spoon. I watched her taking delicate bites, amused. Here I was, slurping away at the noodles, and she was being as precise as a surgeon. "Sometimes you find the things that once did it for you just... don't... anymore."

I studied her face, contemplating her words. "I'm not too young to get it, Sarah."

"No..." she agreed. "But sometimes you just can't tell people things. Sometimes they just have to happen. Life will happen to you. Trust me, it will. No need to hurry it along."

"What if I want to?"

"Everyone says that." Sarah took another sip of wine, looking at me over the rim. "Until things start to happen."

"What things?"

"Just life, sweetie." She sighed, using her napkin and then putting it over her plate, half her food still left there. "You'll get it...when you're older."

I rolled my eyes, mimicking her napkin-over-the-plate gesture. I'd lost my appetite. "Now you really sound like my mother."

"What do you want me to say?" She stood, clearing our plates but leaving the wine glasses. "That I can give you a map?"

"I don't want a map..." I stood, too, but didn't follow her to the kitchen. Instead, I went the few steps into the living room, running my fingers over the edges of her furniture. "I just want to be..."

"Unusual?" she supplied, snagging both of our glasses like a professional waitress in one hand, the bottle of wine in the other.

"I don't have the first clue how to be unusual." I flopped down onto the couch in front of the fire.

"No?" Her voice was closer and softer now as she sat on the floor in front of me, her back resting against my crossed legs. "I think you know more than you let on."

"I don't." Her hair was dry now, as was mine. It was silky against my bare legs, and I touched it. Her hair curled around my fingers and she sighed, leaning her head back, her eyes closed. I looked at her in the firelight. It cast shadows, making rippling patterns on her face, her arms, her breasts spilling slightly over her bra, turning her hair and skin a warm, tawny color.

"Sarah, you're right. My life is as boring as they come. I was valedictorian of my high school class—I'm well on my way to graduating summa cum laude from college. Tim and I went to the junior prom together and have been dating ever since. I got into a good sorority—not, you know, the one with old money, but still... My mother always tells everyone, 'She's such a good girl.' And you know what? She's right. I *am* a good girl."

"I bet you are." She smiled, her eyes still closed.

"What do you mean?'

"Nothing."

I saw a glint on her left hand in the fire light as she shifted. "Sarah, why do you wear a ring?"

"Why?" She opened her eyes to look up at me. They were clear, like blue glass. "Because...because I want men to think I'm taken."

"But you're not."

She frowned, closing her eyes again. "That part of me is."

I stroked her hair at her temple, feeling her relax again. "I wish you'd let someone in."

She shook her head, but didn't say anything. I was feeling warm, from the fire, the wine. She looked so fragile and vulnerable, and the words just came out, "You're so beautiful."

"Look who's talking." Her smile touched her eyes, even closed.

"No." I ran a fingertip down her cheek, so soft. "I'm nothing compared to you. Have you seen the way David looks at you? If a guy looked at me that way..."

"Don't say that." She turned around suddenly, so she was kneeling in front of me, her hands on my thighs. "Elizabeth, you're absolutely beautiful. You know that don't you?"

I shook my head. "I can't do to men what you do. They want you. They all do."

"They want what they think they can't have." She touched a finger to my cheek, trailing it up over my nose to my other cheek, and then down to my lips. I held my breath. She fingered my hair, rubbing it, taking a piece of it and touching it to my cheek, tickling, smiling. "What would you say..." she hesitated. I waited, barely breathing, unsure, uncomfortable and yet transfixed. "If I told you.../want you."

I swallowed hard. "You?"

"Me."

I found my voice. It was a little shaky. "I'd say...I'd say...wow...and...thank you..."

She waited and I didn't say anything else. "But?"

"No buts," I whispered. I touched her hair and she turned her face to rest her cheek on my hand. It was warm and flushed. She kneeled up fully and I uncrossed my legs. She was leaning against the couch between my open thighs, her face inches from mine, her eyes searching.

"Can I kiss you?" she barely whispered, her eyes moving to my lips. I nodded, and she touched her mouth to mine, her arms going around me.

I marveled at her softness, her warmth. I was feeling dizzy, and I didn't know if it was from the wine, or from the kiss. My hands ran up her arms, her skin softer than anything I'd ever felt, across her shoulders, to her back, pulling her closer and feeling her breasts press into mine. She moaned against my lips and I opened my mouth wider, kissing her deeply, lost.

There were no more words then, just sensation, the texture of her tongue, her nails tracing lightly up my back. She let her mouth trail down my neck, nuzzling me gently, making me lean my head back. Nibbling, biting a little, her teeth sending shivers down my arms, she held my hips in her hands and pulled me forward on the couch, so far that I slid slowly off the edge and into her lap. I opened my eyes in wonder, feeling her thighs against mine, looking down at her face, and she was staring at my breasts.

"Beautiful." She kissed the tops of my breasts over my bra, covering them with light, delicious little kisses. Her hands slid behind my back, and she undid the hooks, sliding the straps down my shoulders and off. She hesitated for a moment, looking, and I watched her, a thrill going through me when she moaned and pressed her cheek against my breast, taking my nipple in her mouth.

I whimpered then, arching my back, my hands buried in her mass of blonde hair, trembling as her mouth ran from one nipple to the other. They were pink and hard, and watching her tiny tongue sneak out to taste them made me gasp and writhe in her lap, wrapping my legs around her waist.

My hands explored her back, and I undid her bra almost without thinking, wanting to feel the smooth skin underneath. Her sharp intake of breath when I did made me shiver and I ground my hips slowly against hers, involuntarily, needing to move. I felt her breath coming faster, hot on my breasts, as she licked underneath each one.

She eased me back onto the floor. The rug was soft underneath me, and I laid there, my thighs open, my arms thrown above my head, watching her look down at me. It was an incredible feeling, seeing her explore my body with her eyes, the hunger there growing.

She placed her hands on my sides and leaned over me, kissing my stomach. She pressed her cheek against my navel, rubbing it there, turning her head to dip her tongue into it, flicking gently. I moaned and bit my lip, feeling her hard nipples brushing my thighs as she kissed lower. Her lips were so soft, her breath warm, and my panties were gone in a whisper.

I was suddenly afraid, seeing her there, so close to my sex. She was looking at it, greedy, her hands on my now trembling thighs.

I think she felt my tension because she whispered, "Lizzie, shhh it's okay..." although I hadn't said a word.

She used her tongue to gently part my lips, moving it from side to side, starting lower and moving deliciously upward. I moaned out loud when she reached my clit, throbbing against her skilled tongue, and she moved the flesh gently, easily, the friction building up.

It was too good. I was so excited, my breathing shallow and fast as I moved in rhythm with her mouth. She put her hands on my hips to hold me still, working faster with her tongue, making little noises to urge me on, and that... oh, that sent me over.

"Oh Sarah!" I reached for her as I came, and her hands clenched mine, so tight, her tongue kneading my clit as I shuddered against her. She stopped, pressing her tongue flat against it, a tender bit of flesh now, and I groaned, wiggling. She moved up my body, cupping my sex in her whole hand and pressing hard, making me gasp.

When she lay beside me, I could see my wetness on her mouth, her chin. I touched my finger to her lips, spreading my juices, and lifted it slowly, deliberately, to my mouth. She let out a sigh as she watched me, slowly sliding a finger inside me. I closed my eyes for a moment, feeling her move it gently in and out.

I opened my eyes when I felt her hand move away, and she lifted her finger to my mouth. I let her spread it on my lips, and then sucked her finger greedily into my mouth, making her moan. I leaned in and kissed her, rolling her to her back.

I stopped for a moment to look at her, really look at her, almost in awe. Her breasts were smaller than mine, perfectly rounded, her nipples pink like mine. I traced a finger down her chest, sliding it up across the mound of her breast, toward the peak of her nipple. I circled it slowly, watching the skin purse as she responded.

She moaned, squirming, and I looked at her, her eyes half closed, her breath coming faster, and that did it...I took her other nipple in my mouth. It was soft, like velvet against my tongue at first, and I licked it until it was like a pebble between my lips.

I moved slowly onto her, and she accepted my weight, pulling me close. Her hands moved in my hair, stroking my back. I slipped down her body, kissing her stomach, so flat and smooth, licking the indentation of her waist, her hipbone. She shuddered as I ran my tongue along her skin just above the elastic band of her panties. They were white, and I pulled back to look, seeing the wetness there. She hooked her thumbs in them, sliding them down, and I helped her, moaning when I saw the dark blonde triangle of hair between her legs.

I hesitated, unsure... I'd never done this before, and while I thought I knew what to do—at least, I knew what felt good for me—I wasn't sure how to proceed. She looked down at me, licking her lower lip. I felt her heat radiating against my cheek, breathing in her musky odor.

She slid a hand down and opened her lips, touching her clit with her finger, showing me where she wanted my tongue. I reached out to nudge her finger aside and she gasped, her hips bucking up slightly as I moved my tongue slowly against the side of her clit. Her response emboldened me, and I dipped my tongue lower into the folds, sliding inside of her, really tasting her. She tasted slightly different, but light and fresh, and I swallowed. The taste lingered on my tongue and in my throat.

"Please," she whispered, and the sound of her voice affected me.

I slipped my tongue back up to where I knew she wanted it, focusing on the tiny bud of her clitoris, feeling it harden. Her tiny cries spurred me on. She purred like a kitten at first, squirming against my mouth, catching my rhythm and responding. Her hands found my hair, her fingernails lightly grazing my scalp, sending shivers down my spine.

Licking her excited me. I felt the wetness on my thighs, my clit throbbing. I squeezed my legs together tight as her moans grew louder, her hips moving frantically. I moaned against her clit, making guttural noises deep in my throat. She gasped and came hard, shuddering, calling my name and pushing her hips up to meet my flickering tongue.

"Oh Lizzie, Lizzie, Lizzie," she whispered over and over, reaching for me.

I slid up to her and she pulled my mouth to hers, tasting herself on my tongue, slowly licking her juices off my chin, my neck, rolling me onto my back. She let her hand wander over my body as I looked up at her, her fingertips barely touching me. She propped herself on her elbow and smiled.

"You're beautiful," she said softly.

I closed my eyes, feeling her fingertips moving over me, and I believed her.

* * * *

"Hey…"

Her voice was calling from far away, and I opened my eyes to her navel, the taste of her still thick and warm in my throat, sweet honey.

"Lizzie, it's after midnight. Is someone going to be worried about you?" My eyes found hers in the firelight.

"Hmmm, parents. Whereza phone?" I asked, my voice thick. She reached behind her toward the end table, but couldn't quite reach. I reluctantly shifted my weight to allow her to get it, instantly missing the feel of her body against mine. I sat up, blinking, clutching my knees, suddenly too aware of my skin.

"Guess we fell asleep," she whispered, handing me the cordless phone. I was instantly flushed as I looked at the tips of her nipples, growing harder as I watched, probably just the transition from asleep to awake, from cuddled, fleshy warmth to out-of-bed shivers.

"Guess so," I whispered back, our eyes meeting again. I dropped mine and cleared my throat, dialing in the dimness. Ringing. And ringing.

"Are you okay?" Sarah whispered, running a finger against the fine hairs along my forearm.

I nodded. "Yeah." I wasn't quite sure *what* I was. Then I looked at her again and smiled. "Why are we whispering?" I whispered.

She laughed, softly still, as if we might wake some invisible presence. "I don't know!"

"Lizzie?" It was my mother, sleepy but sure.

"Yeah." There was my voice! "Listen, I'm at Sarah's house. Sarah from work. I'm going to stay over, okay?"

"Call me in the morning." She was already falling back to sleep. "Love you, 'night."

"Love you, too, 'night," I replied, our standard goodbye. I was startled by Sarah's expression as I handed her the phone. "What?"

She looked a little sad, a little surprised as she hung up the phone and turned back to me. She shifted herself so she was turned towards me, her posture mimicking mine, hugging her knees to her breasts. My eyes quickly dipped down those long, tawny-colored thighs and caught a glimpse of the soft, fuzzy patch at their union. I felt the world slip sideways when I saw how slightly open and still glistening she was, remembering the feel and taste of her in my mouth. I felt a familiar flicker in my lower belly.

"What?" I asked again, still seeing that expression, slightly taken aback, on her face.

"I just seduced a girl who still tells her mother 'I love you' before she goes to bed at night," Sarah said with a small snort. "Wow. What was I thinking?" She shook her head at the fire.

And like that it was gone, the liminal space we'd been in since we both startled awake, that sleepy, not-quite-real place. I reached behind me onto her couch and pulled a blanket from the corner, slipping it over my shoulders.

"I should probably get my clothes and go home," I said finally, not looking at her, drawing the blanket around me and pretending to shiver. The fire was too warm for me to really be cold.

Finally, I couldn't stand it, and turned slightly to see her. Her chin rested on her knees and her eyes were warm and full of something I couldn't quite grasp. Okay, fine, so she wasn't going to say anything. I stood up, pulled the blanket around me, and went to step around her. She touched my thigh and I stopped, looking down the waterfall of blanket, seeing her arm disappearing at the wrist underneath it, feeling the warmth of her palm on my thigh, not grasping, not stroking, just a solid, gentle pressure telling me to stop. So I did.

"Elizabeth." She breathed it, out and in— like she was inhaling me with the sound of my name. My knees actually felt weak when

I felt her fingertips move and shift slightly against the soft, sensitive skin of my inner thigh. She didn't say what I wanted to hear—she didn't say I'm sorry I hurt your feelings, that I implied you might be too young for me, that I might be saying I regret doing this. She didn't say that...but she did.

She said, "I want you to stay in my bed tonight. Will you?"

I swallowed. Her eyes and mouth were soft, her hair a golden halo in the firelight. I just nodded. And she took me to her bed.

Chapter Two

I couldn't stop. Once we started, I just couldn't stop. And I didn't tell Tim. I tried, a few times, after one of our quick and fumbling encounters in the back of his Firebird, to tell him about the sweet and magical and amazing thing I'd discovered with Sarah. I loved Tim—he was kind and thoughtful and he tried very hard to please me—but we'd been having sex for over a year and I still hadn't once had an orgasm in his presence.

Since my relationship with Sarah began, I'd asked myself more than once if I might be gay instead of just bi... but my love for a hard cock and, more importantly, men, simply made that impossible. Still, I didn't think of my relationship with Sarah as "cheating" on Tim. How could he possibly compete? It was like apples and oranges. Where he was hard, she was soft—there was just no comparison to be made. They gave me such different things.

But I admit, it became problematic. Sarah wanted more and more of me, and I wanted to give her what she wanted. I couldn't seem to say no to her, and all of a sudden I found myself doing and saying things I'd never imagined myself doing or saying.

Like the time we spent all day sunbathing on her apartment roof. I say we, but it was really Sarah who was slowly turning a beautiful golden brown. I was slathered with sunscreen and sitting under an umbrella, my pale skin too sensitive to ever tan. Then we reclined in the hot August night, talking for hours, and we made love so long and so hard neither of us cared when it started to rain and our moans were drowned out by the sound of storm. I couldn't get enough of her, or she of me. I'd never had anything or anyone like Sarah before. The whole thing was intoxicating.

She asked me about my fantasies. No one had ever asked me that, and I actually told her... although I later discovered the intensity and risk of my fantasies were a playful and innocent kitten to her sleek and stalking panther! She indulged my desires...to dress her up, like a living Barbie doll, in garter belts (oh, my fascination with straps!) and stockings, tight-cinched corsets and even crotchless panties. (The trip to the local "Lover's Lane" for those started with a giggling girls shopping trip, but ended much more seriously with my tongue exploring her for hours past those ever dampening lacy edges.) And then, eventually, she asked me to indulge her fantasies.

How could I say no?

It was almost a month before Sarah opened her toy chest and let me explore a side of my sexuality I wasn't even aware existed. A month of slow exploration, of long days at work where I was afraid the sexual tension between us could be felt by everyone, and nights where I began to vocalize, moving from tiny kitten mews to shameless cries of pleasure. I was lost, and I was trying hard to keep up the pretenses with everyone—Tim, my mom, getting ready for college in the fall—but I really had abandoned them all for Sarah.

We spent part of one memorable night in the coffeehouse, where Sarah was reading some of her erotic poetry for open-mic night—and I couldn't help but squirm a little in my seat when she read the one about our first time together. I just hoped it was dark enough no one saw the slow heat spreading across my cheeks and down my chest and belly. I don't think I'd ever wanted her more—except maybe the first time we'd been together. Her poetry made the audience breathless.

I saw an older man near me surreptitiously rubbing himself through his jeans under the table. That made me even wetter, knowing he wanted her, that even in the dimness I could see the outline of his cock and knew how much he wanted to slide it into the sweetness which would be flooding all over my tongue in the space of an hour. I couldn't believe how exciting it was to see her being desired and knowing she was mine.

I was fantasizing about what Sarah and I were going to do together later when, out of the corner of my eye, I saw the coffeehouse door open. I wouldn't have even glanced away from Sarah except something about the figure filling the doorway was familiar, even in the shadows. I let my eyes leave the stage for a moment, ready to dismiss my suspicion, only to have it confirmed—in my body first, with a quick jolt, and then my brain. I recognized David's strong jaw and big shoulders as he moved through the tables.

I felt frozen, like a rabbit caught in the farmer's garden. My first inclination was to sink down in my seat, become invisible, but I knew it was impossible. The place wasn't crowded enough for me to disappear. And David had spotted me. He threaded his way through the tables, his eyes fixed on mine, and I had nowhere to go. I should have lifted my hand in a wave, just acted casual, but something in me wouldn't allow it.

"Sorry I'm late." David slid into the chair next to mine, shrugging off his soft-looking brown leather jacket. I just stared. Was I supposed to be expecting him?

Sarah's voice was like liquid heat, drawing the attention of everyone in the room, and David was no exception. His gaze swept over her, the knee-high boots and short gray skirt, her white blouse parted into a deep V, purposefully revealing the top of her black lace bra underneath. Her hair was pulled up in a sexy-messy pile on top of her head. She was breathtaking, and the heat in David's eyes reflected her beauty. And she spoke the words of her poetry thick and sexy, dripping honey:

> *"Can't give a starvin' girl*
> *raw meat right away—*
> *not when she's been pickin' bones.*
> *Hungry baby bird mouth,*

greedy cluck and crow,
don't mean she's ready.
Easy does it baby morsels,
tender bitty nibbles,
a slow and sticky suck.
Girl thinks she knows—
she wants it now.
You know better.
Catch her up and give her
one mouthful at a time,
until her dog-hungry belly
and rattle-boned body
can meet that appetite—
then, you can feed her craving,
and let that laid-away
trickling of your love
now flood her eager mouth."

Sarah's voice faded to a full round of applause. I curled my thumb and finger between my lips and whistled, earning a flush and a wink from Sarah as she folded her notebook, took a brief bow, and slipped off the stage. David stood as she approached our table, holding out a chair next to him for her.

"That was amazing." He leaned over the table to give her the compliment as she ignored the chair he'd pulled out for her and slid into the one next to me. "I'm sorry I was late—I would have liked to hear more."

I looked quizzically at Sarah, and her hand squeezing my thigh reassured me. "I could have killed Don for making that announcement at the office. Like I want all of my employees to know I write poetry?"

"Erotic poetry at that," I offered with an evil grin. Sarah shot me a withering look and I stuck my tongue out at her.

David shrugged, leaning back in his chair. "Are you ashamed of it?"

Sarah raised an eyebrow in his direction before her eyes wandered toward the counter. "No, I'm not ashamed. But we're talking about a power differential I didn't particularly want to...exploit."

"Exploit?" David cleared his throat and I could tell he was trying not to smile. "And so because I work for you, I'm...what...? Inferior to you?"

"Not the word I'd choose." Sarah shrugged, her eyes meeting his gaze again. "But in this particular situation, you do just happen to be...below me."

"I don't mind a woman on top." He crossed his arms and tilted his head at her, that smile still playing around his lips.

"I bet," Sarah replied with a smirk, rolling her eyes at me. There was some communication going on between them I couldn't quite catch and didn't understand.

David laughed then, a genuine laugh, shaking his head at her. He looked over at me then and winked. "Just because someone isn't in the driver's seat doesn't mean they don't have a license to drive."

Sarah turned to me, casual-like, and asked, "How many hours did you have to drive on your permit before they gave you your license, Lizzie?"

I blinked at her, then at him. "Are...are we still talking in metaphor?"

David laughed again, nudging me under the table with his knee. He leaned in, as if to reassure me, and said, "I've been driving a very long time."

Sarah's hand on my thigh tightened as she looked at David and said, "I'm dying for a drink after all that reading. David, would you mind getting me a diet Coke?"

"Sure." He stood, his eyes still warm. But there was always a light in them when he looked at Sarah. For the longest time, I thought it was something akin to worship, but now I realized it was hunger. He wanted her, almost as much as I did. Maybe more. He didn't look at me the same way at all. "Lizzie, do you want anything?"

I shook my head and he moved between the tables toward the counter.

"You're so mean," I whispered, turning to face Sarah.

She smiled, sliding her hand further up my leg, inching my skirt up. "Gotta do what you're good at."

I glanced back, making sure David was distracted, and then leaned in to whisper, "You're also incredibly sexy."

She grinned. "Gotta..."

I broke her words with a kiss. I'd been dying to kiss her all night, especially after hearing her recite her poetry, every word dripping sex. It dripped from her tongue like honey, hot and sticky and so sweet it made you ache.

"What if David sees us?" Sarah gasped, pushing me away a little—just a little.

"So what if he does?" I grinned, glancing over my shoulder again. He was talking to the barista, leaning on the counter, his foot up on the stool. He looked incredibly sexy, and a wicked thought came into my head and popped out of my mouth before I could even think about it. "Why don't we invite him back to your place?"

Sarah's eyes widened—I was sure, for a moment, I saw real fear in them, but they turned teasing almost immediately, and so did her tone. "Oh no, you don't!"

"Why not?" I teased back, leaning in nuzzle her ear, whispering, "Wouldn't it be hot? You and me pressing up against him..."

"*A* him, maybe," Sarah agreed, her hand sliding further up my thigh—it couldn't go much further, wedged like it was in the crease like that. The thought of being with Sarah *and* a man had my pussy throbbing with lust. "*That* him? Out of the question."

"You know how I love a challenge," I whispered, nibbling on her earlobe, feeling her shiver. God, I loved making her shiver. "How fast can I turn maybe into yes?"

"Not tonight." Sarah's finger nudged the elastic band of my panty leg aside, searching through the soft, red plethora of pubic hair, looking for wetness.

"Why not?" I asked, distracted now by her fingers as they parted my pussy lips under the cover of the table, the darkness making me feel bolder as I spread my legs wider for her.

"Because tonight, you're mine," she insisted, sliding a finger inside of me, making me moan against her neck. "Come on, Lizzie. Let's get out of here."

"But David—" I started to glance over my shoulder again, and Sarah's other hand slipped behind my hair, pulling me in with her palm curled around the nape of my neck, and kissed me—hard.

"Forget about him."

I blinked in surprise as she stood, rubbing her wet fingers—wet with my juices—against my lips. "Him...who?"

She had her hand up my skirt again while she drove us back to her apartment, tugging at my panties and rubbing the moist fabric. She would periodically lift her fingers to my mouth to let me suck them. It reminded me of the dizzying taste and feel of her sex, and I moaned and squeezed my legs together around her hand. I don't know how we made it back without getting into an accident.

It was that night that she opened the chest. She was watching me undress, lying naked already on her bed, when she said, "Lizzie, I have to show you something." I stopped mid-button, curious. "Close your eyes."

I obliged, standing at the end of the bed in nothing but my blue chambray shirt which was unbuttoned to my navel. She slipped a hand under my shirt and cupped my breast as she passed me, thumbing my nipple, and I shivered, feeling it harden immediately. I heard her fumbling around in the room, the air shifting as she walked past me to the far wall—a click, a deep creaking, the sound of Sarah kneeling.

"Open your eyes." She was on her knees next to an open wooden chest, her legs slightly open, her hands resting on her thighs. "My hope chest."

Her smile was mischievous and, indeed, hopeful. It looked exactly like an old hope chest, the kind my grandmother had passed on to my mother, but instead of knitted doilies and linen, this hope chest was full of prurience and supplication. I was transfixed by the contents, almost as if she'd opened a chest of gold. The scent of it alone was alluring, the heavy redolent smell of leather and something deeper, more fully and secretly human.

I slowly sank to my knees beside her and we were motionless for a while, I don't know how long, as I explored the contents with my eyes and she watched me. I felt her gaze on me, and realized I'd stopped breathing. I drew a deep and shaky breath and met her eyes. They were lustful and questioning and something else I'd never seen before and was a little afraid of. I told her so.

"Sarah, I... I'm a little scared."

She nodded. "Yes."

It wasn't so much an acknowledgement of my fear as an affirmation. She wanted this. And there was a part of me that simply couldn't tell her no. She reached into the box without a word and pulled out a black silk scarf. I'd never forget her slipping it over my eyes that first time, tying it behind my head.

"Can you see? Be honest." Her voice had changed completely. It held element of confidence I'd never heard before. It stopped my breath. I couldn't speak. I just shook my head.

"When I ask you a question, I want you to say, 'Yes, Sarah,' or 'No, Sarah.' Do you understand?"

"Yes, Sarah." It was easier than I thought it would be.

"Can you see, Elizabeth?"

"No, Sarah."

"Good. Now stand up."

I struggled to my feet. It was strangely difficult without my sight.

"Good girl...now take off your shirt."

I swallowed hard, managing the few remaining buttons, easing the shirt off my shoulders and letting it fall to the floor. I felt unbelievably exposed and crossed my arms over my breasts. I couldn't see anything, but I could feel her disapproval.

"Ah Lizzie, you should see yourself," she breathed and I felt her fingers brush lightly over my thighs. Then her voice changed again. "Put your hands behind your back," she commanded. I was more reluctant now, but I did it.

"Spread your legs... further... good."

Her hands roughly massaged between my legs, and I felt a cold rush of air when she spread my lips wide for a moment. I wondered if she was inspecting me. That's what it felt like as her hands ran over my body, a little roughly at times, pushing my foot out a little further, turning my shoulder, tilting my head with her hand.

"Mm... yes..." she breathed, her face close to mine now. I felt the warmth of her and remembered how much I'd wanted her tonight. I still wanted her, but my desire seemed secondary to this new feeling in my belly. I had no idea what it was.

"Elizabeth, I don't want you to move. Do you understand?" I nodded. I could tell she was waiting. "Elizabeth?"

Then I remembered.

"Yes, Sarah." I said hastily. The hard sting of her hand on my bottom brought tears to my eyes, more from surprise than pain, and I whimpered.

"Don't move." I didn't. She left the room, and still, I didn't move. What was keeping me there? I wondered. I could walk away if I wanted to. Take off the blindfold, go lay on the bed, call Sarah back in, snuggle and make love and doze. I knew I could, and she would be okay with it.

But this was appealing to me, even as it was strange and uncomfortable and a little humiliating. I could tell it excited her. I heard it in her voice, felt it in the new way she touched me. And I wanted more of that. So I stood still and I waited, legs spread, blindfolded, my hands behind my back.

My other senses seemed heightened without the use of my eyes. I heard her moving around in the other room, going through drawers. She came back in and I stiffened slightly, trying to control my movement, even my breathing. I smelled the sulfur of a match being lit, heard the sound of her shuffling through the chest and, in my mouth, tasted the lingering musk of myself licked from her fingers. I swallowed.

"Find your way to the bed and lie down."

The sound of her voice startled me. I made my way slowly, my knees hitting the edge before I crawled onto the bed.

"On your belly," she instructed.

On my stomach, the sheets cool under my skin, I was now very aware of the wet throbbing between my legs. Oh God, this was so exciting. I could almost feel her eyes on me.

"Spread your legs."

I opened them. She knelt behind me, spreading my legs even wider with her knees.

"Up." She put her hand between my legs, cupping my sex and lifting slightly. I raised my bottom in the air, my breasts still pressing into the bed, the blindfold shifting slightly when I turned my head. I wanted her to touch me. I wanted her hands, her mouth, her soft, skilled tongue. My thighs trembled.

"Touch yourself," she said.

I reached between my legs and slid my fingers through my wetness, immediately heading for my aching little clit.

"Open yourself for me."

I whimpered, spreading my lips with my fingers.

"Good girl." I heard her breathe in deeply, inhaling me. "Your pussy is very swollen, Elizabeth... and you're wet all over... do you feel that?" She rubbed wetness into my thighs.

"Yes, Sarah."

"I think you might be enjoying this... are you enjoying this, Elizabeth?"

"Yes, Sarah, oh yes." I moaned, arching my back slightly. And it was true. I was beyond excited now. I was lost in some other world where lust was the only thing that existed. My want was enormous.

"Good." She suddenly seemed distracted. I used the muscles deep inside, squeezing, feeling the sensation in my throbbing clit.

She chuckled. "Brat!" When I felt her hand sting my bottom again, I yelped. "Tempting me?"

"Yes, Sarah." I felt my cheeks flush.

"Put your fingers in your pussy."

I probed higher, finding that entrance, opening it for a moment, knowing she was watching, and then slid my fingers in deep. I heard her sharp intake of breath.

"Finger yourself."

I did. Slowly at first, remembering how it felt to have a cock inside, so much bigger, harder, filling me. My fingers always seemed so inadequate. But the motion, my fingers delving deep as I rocked, my thumb against my clit, made me moan and thrust harder. Sarah's breath came faster. I wondered if she had her fingers in her own pussy and the thought spurred me on.

"Stop!"

I groaned, dropping my hand to the bed, my fingers soaking. I waited. The anticipation was exquisite. Finally, I felt her fingers parting me, exploring the fleshy folds, finding my clit for a moment and rubbing, then back to my slit again, slowly up and down. It drove me to distraction.

"Your pussy is so beautiful," she whispered. I felt her reverence. I nearly came the minute she leaned in and kissed my clit, sucking it gently into her mouth. Her tongue flickered over it for a moment, then slid up through the slippery folds to drink me in. I moaned softly, pressing back against her, and she steadied me with her hands on my hips.

"I have a surprise for you," she murmured, and I stiffened, unsure. "Relax." She stroked my bottom and thighs. I felt myself open up a little more. She slid a finger inside of me, then two, pumping in and out at an easy pace. I was just catching her rhythm when she slid it into me...big and hard, so much less pliant than a real cock, absolutely filling me.

"Oh my God!" I gasped. "Sarah!"

"Yes," she murmured, easing it in deeper. "I'm going to fuck you."

That's when I realized the hard cock inside of me was strapped around her waist. I felt her thighs against mine, her hands grabbing my hips. It was all the way inside me now, as deep as it could go, almost uncomfortably huge and a bit unforgiving. She shifted her weight and the cock inside of me pressed against the smooth wall of my pussy, making me arch my back to meet her movement.

"Now tell me," she demanded.

"Tell you...?" I was breathless, unable to focus.

"Tell me you want it."

"Oh God, yes, Sarah! I want it!"

"More?" She pressed in deeper, just when I thought it wasn't possible. I bit my lip.

"Yes!" I hissed. She started easing away, taking the cock with her, and I panicked. "No, no, I want it, please, please!"

"What do you want, Elizabeth? Ask for what you want."

"I..." Now I was suddenly reticent, unable to say it. I whimpered. She pulled the cock further out, so just the tip rested at the entrance of my pussy. "No, please," I whispered.

"Ask for what you want," she repeated.

The silence stretched, and I found myself humbled, afraid to say the words, afraid of the power of my appetite and what it might say about me if I spoke it out loud. Her fingers slowly eased their way up from the cock, spreading the wetness through the crack of my ass, probing a little there, and I shivered.

"Please..." I pleaded.

"Yes," she said. "Ask for what you want."

"Ohhh God..." I trembled, so hungry. Her weight shifted, and I felt the tip of that big, hard cock start to move. I arched my back instinctively to keep it there. "Oh Sarah, please, fuck me, fuck me!" I begged, unabashed now, all thought gone, consumed completely with a deep longing to be filled.

Her thrust was her response, and it drove me down onto the bed. She was fucking me, my Sarah, with an enormous cock between her soft, supple thighs. She reached underneath me, to steady me, maybe, or for leverage, and also, I discovered, to find my clit with her fingers. She rubbed with a steady motion as she pushed into me, over and over. My nipples were hard on the bed, rubbing as she rocked me. My hair hung in my face, covering the blindfold, which now seemed like a relief, an excuse to stay inwardly focused on the overwhelming sensation.

"Tell me," she said again, and this time I didn't hesitate.

"Fuck me, Sarah! Fuck me *hard*!" My voice had changed, became someone else's as I felt my climax building. I realized in a moment of panic that I'd never come with anything inside of me before.

"Harder?" She pushed deep.

"Yes, yes, hard! *Hard*!" I gasped, feeling that deep tickle I knew meant I was only moments away from flooding all over that cock.

"Come for me." She rubbed faster, oh God, exactly there, exactly right, pressing in deep and staying there as she worked my clit.

"Oooooh yes, Sarah, I'm coming!" I gasped, the muscles of my pussy clamping down on that hard cock, buried to the hilt, meeting hard resistance. I spread my legs wider, letting her hand rock me and take me there, wave after delicious wave making me buck and moan.

She reached down further and cupped my mound, pressing, and I sighed, loving that she knew how good that felt, feeling my flesh pulse against her hand. She leaned back and slowly eased out of me. The difference was startling.

"Elizabeth," she whispered, and her voice sounded almost shaky.

"Mmmm," was my response, still lost. She reached behind my head and undid my blindfold.

"Elizabeth, roll over," she said. I did. "Open your eyes."

And my first sight was Sarah, oh my God, between my legs, all blonde hair and golden skin, with that huge (black!) cock strapped across her crotch! She saw my reaction in my eyes and smiled. She made her way slowly up my body, until she was kneeling across my breasts, the cock resting there.

"You came so good," she murmured, running her hand through my hair, brushing it away from my forehead, my cheeks. She took the cock in her hand, still wet with my juices, and rubbed it over my breasts, my nipples. Then she placed the tip of it on my lips.

"Suck," she instructed.

I took it, greedy, sucking my come off that massive black cock. She watched me, her eyes hungry. She pressed in further, further, until I nearly choked on the length as she watched it disappear into my mouth. Then she reached to her side and undid something, and the cock was gone. She moved further up, steadying herself on the headboard, spreading her thighs and moving her pussy directly over my mouth.

My mouth was open, my tongue reaching in anticipation. Unexpectedly, she reached down and put her hand behind my neck, not so much settling herself onto my tongue as lifting my mouth to her pussy. I licked her eagerly, hungry and wanting to please her. She lifted up a little, so she was just out of my reach, my face already wet with her.

"Put your tongue out," she demanded. I reached with my tongue. "Now... hold still."

"Yes, Sarah," I said before reaching my tongue out again, and a brief, satisfied smile flickered on her face before getting lost in lip-biting pleasure as she used my stiff, still tongue to bring herself to climax, rocking back and forth on my face. "Oh God, oh fuck, Lizzie," she moaned, and I nearly drowned in her juices when she came, shuddering and pressing me hard against her pussy.

"Yes, yes, yes," I murmured, rubbing my chin and cheeks over her wetness.

"Don't move," she breathed.

Even in this moment of complete abandon, she was still in control. She moved off of me, taking the cock with her. "Close your eyes," she instructed.

I did as I was told, still seeing her kneeling above me with that hard cock, feeling her moist flesh in my mouth, lost completely in who and what she'd become to me. I heard her doing something in the bathroom at the sink, then she came back into the room. More shuffling, the slow creak of the chest lid I would come to know so well my clit would throb in immediate Pavlovian response every time I heard it.

Then Sarah was back in bed, pulling me to her in the way we liked to lay, my head tucked in under her chin, resting on the softness of her breast.

"Cold?" she asked. I shook my head. I couldn't have been more warm, all over.

"Does your mother know about the collection you have in your hope chest?" I asked coyly. She chuckled.

"You haven't seen the half of it, sweetie." She kissed my forehead. "But you will." I shivered, and not from cold.

"Sarah..." I said after a moment. "You do like men, yes?" We'd had this discussion before. She nodded, her eyes closed, already drifting. I stopped, unable to go further, unsure.

She sensed it and opened her eyes. "Ask for what you want."

I'd been thinking about the differences of being with Tim and Sarah, and I'd always thought I would be one of those women who just wouldn't ever have an orgasm with a man. Maybe I was too inhibited with them, or maybe it was just that Tim was so inexperienced, and often too interested in his own pleasure to notice mine.

But now, after this...

"I've never come with a cock inside me before," I confessed.

Her eyebrow went up but she didn't say anything.

I flushed. "I liked it."

A small smile. Encouraged, I said, "I really liked it...but I don't think I could do it without you."

Now both eyebrows were up and she was looking at me, bemused.

"Ask for what you want," she said again, rubbing my jaw line with her finger.

"I want to be with a man...with you," I blurted, moving to tuck my head under her chin again, hiding. There were no words for a long time. Finally I had to inquire, "Sarah?"

"Not Tim," she said definitely.

"No!" I was horrified. "Someone else... I don't know who..."

Again, silence. I waited, hopeful.

"I can't say no to you...and you know it," she murmured, pulling me close.

"Does that mean yes?"

She touched my lips with her fingertip and then kissed me. "Yes."

I spent the whole night with her that night, which I couldn't often do, and we slept snuggled together until the first bit of light started seeping between her blinds. I woke up once in the middle of the night and found her sleeping curled on her side, her face soft and relaxed, and tried to imagine sharing her with a man. Yes, I wanted it. But I also knew that you had to be careful what you wished for.

Chapter Three

Everywhere I looked, I saw a partner for Sarah and I to invite into our bedroom. And I was thinking of it as "our bedroom" now, too. I couldn't kid myself anymore, that this was just an experimental thing, that we were two girls just having fun together. It had become much more than that, for both of us.

And Tim knew it on some level, although he didn't know how to say it. In fact, I think people at work were beginning to suspect as well. David had been watching us since the beginning, always hungry for Sarah. She claimed not to notice, but I couldn't help see his eyes following her when she passed his cubicle, scanning the short hemline of her skirt, the sweet indentation of her belted waist, the swell of her breasts in her peasant blouse. I knew he watched us together when he hung around to "clean up" his paperwork while we talked and laughed and flirted in the back office, his eyes alight with something that made my belly flicker in response.

Tim, on the other hand, didn't like to even hear her name mentioned and whenever he picked me up from work and she was around, they faced off rather coolly, the tension between them palpable. He would always make some comment as we left—

often loud enough for her to hear him— "That one's trouble." I shrugged it off and hoped he had no real idea...but they say love is blind.

The other complication was college in the fall, which was fast approaching. Summer was slipping away from all of us, and I would be back at school two hundred miles away with Tim... without Sarah.

I'd been re-thinking even going back, that's how caught up I was, but Sarah would laugh softly and nudge me whenever I mentioned it and reply, "Time to be a grown-up, Lizzie..."

The comment inevitably—and I think purposefully—distanced me enough from her to make me forget the idea of staying home. Each day found me closer and yet further away from her. We continued to have our play dates, as I liked to call them. Ah, what my mother might have said if she'd known I would transform the phrase she used in reference to the scheduled times I'd gone to play with friends when I was five into the term I used now for the sticky, sweaty, sex sessions I was having with Sarah! Each time she made it a new discovery, a different experience. Sarah didn't ask me about my sex life with Tim, and I didn't ask her about her sex life separate from me...although I wondered if she had one.

One Saturday morning, after she'd allowed me to slowly and sweetly fuck her to a shuddering climax with one of the dildos from the toy box—something I discovered I loved and often begged to do to her!—I was cleaning off the toy (always the job of the fuck-er as opposed to the fuck-ee) when I found condoms in the bathroom closet.

I was immediately flooded with both jealousy and lust. It was a strange combination that reminded me how much I wanted to share that with her, to add something, more to the point *someone*, to our sex life.

We'd been to bars and scoped out guys, and we'd taken many of them home with us in our imaginations and fantasies. We would dance for hours together, often finding an unsuspecting but grateful guy to sandwich between our damp and writhing bodies, our eyes meeting in lust and keen awareness.

She loved to play the fantasy with me later, the memory of the music still pounding in my body, recalling a hard denim-covered cock rubbing against my backside. She'd strap on that magnificent black dildo and handle me roughly, asking,

"Do you want his cock in you, Lizzie? Tell me how much you want it..."

But we had yet to really take a man home. It was when I found the condom I made up my mind, I think, to make it a reality, in whatever way I could. No more playing, no more just flirting and driving each other to distraction with the idea.

And of course, the man we ended up "taking home" was probably the most obvious choice, although I'd never really imagined it would happen with him. I always thought it would be one of the younger guys with their piercings or tattoos who we slowly flirted away from their girlfriends at the club. I really never anticipated that it would be with David, or that it would fall into place so easily one Friday night, not unlike the first night I'd been with Sarah, or that the results of that night would be so bittersweet.

It was the end of the work week. Sarah and I were planning on going out to the club. It was only two more weeks until school started, and that weighed heavily on both of us, although we didn't talk about it. Tim was busy, going to a bachelor party for his best friend, although the thought of getting married at our age was anathema to me.

I was telling Sarah that when David came into the back office.

"She's only nineteen, Sarah. Can you even imagine?" I sat on the edge of the desk, my shoes off, swinging my bare feet and noticing her looking at my legs admiringly, not for the first time today, under my green and blue plaid skirt. I'd worn it specifically for clubbing, along with the white blouse that made it look the typical "school girl" uniform. I was determined to bring home a guy tonight, and I'd told her so. She'd eyed my outfit, laughed, and then said, "That'll do it."

"Can you imagine?" I asked again, punctuating my statement with a nudge.

"Maybe she's pregnant," she replied distractedly, chewing on the end of her pen and peering through her reading glasses at some report.

"No one gets married because they're pregnant anymore." I rolled my eyes. "I know a girl who had nine abortions. *Nine.* Seriously."

Sarah did look up then, her eyes showing surprise. "Well...not everyone can make that decision."

"I guess." My nonchalance seemed to irk her even more. She turned almost imperceptibly away, just a slight tilt of her shoulder, and went back to her report.

I watched David gathering up his paperwork through the two-way glass. I knew he was listening, even though he couldn't see us. The office door was open.

"Is that a real wedding ring?" I nudged her again with my foot, tugging her skirt upwards with my toe.

"You know it isn't." She flipped one of the pages of the report so hard it tore.

"It looks real." I leaned in to look at it as she clutched the paper in her hand. "Did you go out and buy it?"

"Not exactly." Sarah turned and yanked open a drawer, digging through the tray of pens.

"Where did you get it?"

She slammed the door shut, a yellow highlighter clenched in her fist. "Someone gave it to me."

"What someone?" I knew I was pushing it—even for me.

Sarah looked at me, blinking fast, her mouth open but no words coming out. "Lizzie, I've got work left to do."

"Sheesh, avoid much?" I hopped off the desk. "Fine, I'll go talk to David."

She grabbed my arm and sighed. "Sit down."

I did. "Are you mad at me?"

"No." She pulled the cap off the highlighter and drew a fat star next to something on the report. "I'm not mad at you."

I sat on the edge of the desk, watching her, waiting. "So who are you mad at?"

"I'm not mad." She was back to highlighting again.

"And I'm Sister Mary Margaret from Our Holy Virginity."

She laughed then, shaking her head. "Sometimes I don't know what to do with you."

"Just pay attention to me." I stuck my tongue out at her.

"Brat." She smiled, going back to her work.

"Sarah, I'm going back to school in two weeks," I whined. "We don't have much longer. What's more important, me or that stupid report?"

Her eyes flashed as she glanced up at me. "This is life, Lizzie. And trust me, life sucks. And it never stops sucking. Get used to it."

"You're such a bitch." I pouted.

"And you're such a baby." She continued to chew on her pen cap and we sat in silence for a while, Sarah working, me pouting.

"Are we fighting?" I asked.

She smiled up at me. "Do you want to fight?"

"I don't know what I want." I sighed.

"Maybe that's the problem." She traced her fingernail down a line of numbers, distracted again.

"Well I know what I *don't* want."

"Hm?"

I nudged her again. "I don't want to get married before I'm forty."

"You'd better put Tim on a leash, then." Sarah snorted.

"Very funny."

"Nineteen, Sarah!"

"I heard you." She slipped her glasses off and rubbed her eyes. "Stupid people do stupid things. Young people are inherently stupid. And again, I wouldn't rule out the pregnancy idea."

"But—she's   only   nineteen! And...hey...are you calling me stupid?"

"Who's only nineteen?" David had materialized, filling the door frame. I knew the moment I looked at him that he'd overheard us.

"My boyfriend's friend's girlfriend...well, fiancée, I guess," I amended. "They're getting married next weekend. Who in their right mind gets married at nineteen?" I noticed him looking at where my foot was resting on Sarah's thigh, but I didn't move it. She was too busy working again to notice him noticing.

"Nineteen is right about the age when you think you know everything, but you really don't know anything." He moved further into the room, helping himself to the other chair opposite Sarah. He set his surveys down on her desk. "I was only twenty when I got married...trust me, I can believe it." He sighed. Sarah glanced at him for a moment, then at me. David didn't usually talk about his private life.

"You're married?" I was just making conversation. Sarah had told me he was divorced.

"Was married," he corrected.

"How long?" Sarah asked.

I cocked my head at her. I didn't think she'd ever paid this much attention to David. It wasn't just that she'd asked him a personal question—it was that Sarah was showing an actual *interest*.

"Eight years."

I raised my eyebrows. Their eyes were locked, and there was some communication going on between them that I didn't get.

"Kids?" I asked, just for something to say.

"No." He smiled over at me. "She wanted them, but I..." He cleared his throat. "I can't. That was one of the things that broke us up, actually."

"Can't?" I looked at him, puzzled. "Can't have...sex?"

"Lizzie!" Sarah pinched the inside of my thigh, making me yelp. She looked kindly at

David—so kindly, her face didn't even look like Sarah's for a moment there. "He means he's sterile. Probably a low sperm count?"

"That's about right." David nodded and shrugged. "I'm shooting blanks."

"Oh." I rubbed my thigh. It hurt.

"It was the same with us." Sarah revealed. "My ex wanted them, but I couldn't..." I noticed her looking down at the ring she was wearing, and it didn't occur to me for a moment that when she said "her ex," she actually meant ex-*husband*. "I had... well, I was damaged. Pretty much beyond repair. There was no way I could carry a child to term. So he went and married someone else who could."

"I'm sorry, Sarah." David didn't reach out to touch her, but she responded as if he had, her face softening as she looked at him.

"Lizzie, you can close your mouth," she said, not even glancing at me, but smiling a small, knowing smile.

My mouth snapped shut, and I tried not to reveal my hurt. I dropped my foot from her lap. David sensed something going on between the two of us, but his eyes never left her for a moment.

"I know, it hurts, doesn't it?"

It took me a moment to realize, he wasn't talking to me, but to her. She looked at him speculatively, still with the pen cap in her mouth. Finally, she nodded.

"How long?" he asked.

"I got married at twenty-eight...was married for five years. He was..." She groped for the right word. "Self-absorbed."

That put the divorce about two years ago, I calculated.

David nodded, leaning back in his chair. They were looking at each other, and I think she was really seeing him for the first time. With his dark curly hair, big brown eyes and flirtatious nature, she seemed to always dismiss him as a pretty boy. She'd never really given him a chance, and I wondered, looking at the way she was looking at him now, if he reminded her of her ex in other ways. And I wondered if I was going to get the chance to find out.

David seemed to sense her shift, and asked with a small smile, "I suppose it's no use asking you what you're doing tonight?" I don't think I'd ever seen Sarah blush, before or since.

"We were going—" I started, trying to save her.

"To my place to watch movies," Sarah finished. She glanced at me and tapped underneath her chin with her index finger, and once again, I closed my mouth. I knew exactly what she was up to, and while I'd been the one to ask for it, I suddenly wondered what I was in for.

"Wanna come?" Her invitation was warm and genuine. I felt it in my belly at the sound of her voice, and David's eyes were dark with his response.

"Yes," was all he said, and I swallowed hard.

"Great, we'll all make a night of it." She got up to start closing up shop, brushing by him and intentionally—I knew how oh-so-intentionally—letting her hip rub against his shoulder as she reached for the light switch. I slid off the desk. I couldn't do anything now but follow. I didn't realize until later that it was what I'd been doing all along.

Chapter Four

The similarities between the night Sarah and I had first been together were eerie. It served to be quite a bookend to our relationship, I suppose. When the three of us emerged from the building, the sky was dark and had opened up in sheets of rain. We stood huddled in the alcove for a moment, and I gasped and moved instinctively closer to David when lightning struck not too far in the distance. He offered to go get his car and drive us all to Sarah's, but she shook her head.

"No, I don't want to leave my car here," she said. "Hey, Lizzie, why don't you ride with David? You can show him the way to my place, and I'll stop and pick up a movie on the way."

I cocked an eyebrow at her and she just looked at me, steady. Okay, okay, so I was supposed to trust she knew what she was doing. I glanced at David and saw his disappointment at not riding with Sarah. I wondered if he could see mine...or if she could.

"Okay," was all I could say. "We'll see you there?"

"Yep." She slipped off her heels, covered her head with her purse, and bolted for her car. The sight of her bare legs, the flash of skin under her skirt as she fled, her squeal at the stinging rain already soaking through her blouse, were enthralling. I looked over at David and saw the same thing in his eyes. What a pair we were.

"I'll go get my car," he said, not even looking at me. "You wait here." I nodded and watched him walk through the parking lot while I stood in the corner of the alcove, just beginning to shiver. When he pulled up, he reached over and opened the door for me, and I slid inside. Just in the dash to the car door, I was soaked. It was warm and dry in the car, the heat already kicked up. I huddled against the door, my teeth chattering. He looked over at me and chuckled.

"Here," he said kindly, reaching behind the seat and bringing forward his suit coat. "You look like a drowned kitten." I tucked the jacket in around me. He was a big guy—it covered from just under my chin all the way to the middle of my shins—and although the outside was wet, the inside was dry, and brought a little more thankful warmth.

He turned the radio on low, to the alternative station I always listened to, which surprised me. I instructed him slowly, in stages, on how to get to Sarah's, and he followed the directions casually. Other than that we were pretty quiet. He hummed along to the songs, and I stole sideways glances at him in the dimness. His hair was even more curly when wet, it seemed, and in spite of myself, I had a sudden urge to finger one of those curls at the nape of his neck. He pulled up to Sarah's apartment but he left the car running.

"Looks like she's still at the video store," I said.

"Do you have a key?" The awareness in his eyes was unmistakable. *He knew.* I shook my head, denying it, although I did have a key and he probably knew that, too. "Well... I guess we wait, then."

The silence stretched and the rain fell steadily on the car roof. I looked up at the warm squares of apartment windows, wondering at the secret lives in each and if they compared in any way to the drama of my life in the past few months. I reached over to turn the radio up and he didn't object.

Oh Sarah, what was I thinking? I mused, finding her window, lowly lit on the second floor, the balcony glistening in the rain. *I love you and he loves you and how in the world is this ever going to make any of us happy?* I almost expected her to come out onto the balcony, a modern-day Juliet. Romeo was here, sitting next to me in his Lumina...but who was I? There was no part for me to play here.

A streak of lightning followed a powerful crack of thunder so swiftly they seemed simultaneous. I gasped, clutching at David's sleeve. Storms always made me both exhilarated and uneasy with their sheer force, but this was so abrupt it more than startled me—I admit it, I panicked.

The rain, which had been slowing a bit, instantly became a deluge, pouring over the windshield like a waterfall. Thunder rumbled again, and another bolt of lightning hit the ground in the middle of the field next to the apartment building. I gasped and jumped again. David instinctively put his arm around me and pulled me closer.

Then the hail started. The angry, tin-roof sound was deafening, and we watched as it hit the windshield and bounced off like ping-pong balls into the parking lot and onto the grass. It was surreal. Another clap of thunder had me whimpering and hiding my face against his shirt. He stroked my wet hair, cradling my head under his chin.

He intuitively understood, I think, my reaction to the power of the storm. And I was thinking of Sarah, out in this by herself. Then I realized he probably was, too.

"Shh." He comforted me, his voice soothing and low. I hadn't realized until he said something that I was still whimpering. "It's letting up. It'll be over soon."

He was right. The deeper sound of the hail was slowing, replaced by the lighter sound of rain. As the storm ebbed, I slowly became aware of his body against mine. He'd pulled me in tight to comfort me, and we sat thigh to thigh, my cheek resting on his damp shirt. The steady sound of his heartbeat calmed me.

I became aware of a few dark curly hairs framed by the edges of his white button down shirt where he'd undone the top two after taking off his tie—obviously all before I got into the car. I hadn't noticed before. His hand was still in my hair, and I heard and felt him inhale deeply, breathing in the scent of me. I closed my eyes for a moment and simply let myself feel him, solid and warm, his breathing a little quicker now, his hand moving to my shoulder and squeezing slightly. It felt good. More than that—it felt right.

I tilted my head to look up at him, the outline of his jaw, the curve of his mouth. He met my eyes and the power of what I saw there made me weaker and more afraid than I'd been a few minutes ago during the storm. I flushed with anticipation and he smiled, his eyes even darker, wolfish in their sudden hunger. How had we gone from me huddling against the door, jealous and petulant and as far away from him as I could get, to this warm and intimate embrace? Ten minutes ago I thought the distance between us was immeasurable. A thunderclap later, I realized, the actual distance was just a tug and slide across the leather seat and the inner distance was really much, much less than that.

Both of us startled when Sarah knocked briefly on the window and continued on to the apartment's main door. We both quickly and a little guiltily untangled ourselves, and I silently handed his jacket back. I saw Sarah silhouetted in the doorway, waiting for us.

"Still raining. Why don't you wear it in?" he offered, slipping it around my shoulders. He pulled my hair out from under the collar in a sweeping motion, a sweet and intimate gesture. The feel of his hand brushing against the back of my neck made me close my eyes for a brief second in response.

"Thanks. C'mon, let's run for it."

It was still pouring when we opened our respective doors and bolted toward Sarah. We met at the front of the car, and he grabbed my hand mid-run and pulled me, faster, toward our end point. We were both laughing when we reached her, and I doubled over, a sharp stitch in my side, as we crowded in the entryway. Sarah smiled and looked back and forth between us, seeing David search my eyes out as we caught our breath and noting the connection there. In that instant I realized what she'd done, sending me to ride with him, and I marveled at her intuition.

We found our way to her apartment, which was as familiar to me as home now. Sarah told David to make himself comfortable and we went to change. Her work clothes gave way to a pair of blue sweats and a U of M t-shirt. I noticed she wasn't wearing a bra, and her nipples were still hard from her run through the rain.

She offered me her robe while my clothes dried. I was struck with an eerie sense of déjà vu as I slipped on her old terrycloth robe, pale pink and fraying at the edges, the most un-sexy thing I could imagine. I sighed as I tossed my blouse and skirt—which I'd been so sure would entice home some young hottie tonight—into the dryer.

Sarah slipped her hands under my robe before I tied it, one hand kneading the sensitive flesh of my belly just above my pubic hair, the other slipping behind me to my lower back. I knew everything I was feeling showed in my eyes because I could see it reflected in her own, and she kissed my eyelids closed and then kissed my mouth, a gentle, tender and reassuring kiss.

I breathed a shaky sigh and she spent a moment feathering kisses on the sweet spot on my neck, just below and behind my ear, which she knew made me instantly wet. Her hand on my belly kneaded lower, slipping under the elastic of my panties and through my pubic hair.

I heard and felt her breath quicken with my own when she found and parted my pussy lips, slipping two fingers through my slit, one on each side of my already swollen clit. I moaned when she wiggled her fingers and she stopped the sound with her mouth against mine. I wondered at her boldness, and glanced toward the door, which was open, but out of the line of sight of the living room where we'd left David.

Her two fingers moved easily—so wet already!—and found the thin and sensitive sheath of skin covering my clit. The sensation was exquisite, her touch practiced and deft. She applied just a small amount of pressure to the tiny bud of flesh, not so much directly on my clit, just allowing that sweet layer of skin to do the work, rubbing it in slow and easy circles with the flat of her fingers.

Her hand on my lower back allowed her to guide me, support me, and I let my head fall back, pushing my hips forward to meet her hand. She pushed me back against the wall, making faster circles now, easing me gently upward. She pressed her mouth to my ear so I could feel her breath and I whimpered. My nipples rubbed against the terrycloth as I rocked my hips, and I sighed when she slipped both fingers down and pressed them into me as deeply as she could.

"He's got a big, hard cock for you, Lizzie," she whispered, stretching me open even further with both fingers, and then slowly sliding in a third. My eyes flew open at the sensation and the thought. "Do you want it?" She moved her fingers in and out of me, deeply. I rocked rhythmically with her, trying not to make too much noise.

"Do you want that cock, Lizzie? Tell me," she demanded, fucking me harder. My eyes were slits, my mouth open, my head back. I imagined his cock sliding into me like that and flushed at the intensity of my own greed.

"Yes, yes, Sarah, please," I begged in a whisper. She pulled her fingers quickly from me and rubbed them against my mouth. The smell and taste of me made me suck and lick her fingers eagerly. She watched, delighted, her mouth making a perfect little "o" that I ached to kiss.

"Good girl," she encouraged. She pulled my robe closed and tied it, a little roughly. "I rented 'Henry and June.'" Her eyes were dancing, and I groaned. Sarah and I had watched it just three weeks ago, an incredibly erotic story of the love affair between Anais Nin and Henry Miller, and we'd had to stop the movie twice to play! I smiled to myself. Poor David didn't have a clue what he was in for tonight...

I didn't see David at first as we came out and Sarah angled for the kitchen. I noticed he'd started a fire—gone were the days when men had to actually use wood and matches, now they just flipped a switch! Then I saw him kind of squatting in front of it, warming his hands, and I imagined, hoping to dry his clothes a bit. I was stopped by the sight of him, his presence completely filling the room, the firelight flickering in his eyes and against his palms.

Sarah moved past me, carrying something. "Here, go put these on," she urged, handing him a pile of clothes. "My ex was about your size, I think." He stood to accept them from her, and I noticed how their hands lingered for a moment, how his eyes sought hers, and I don't know if he saw or felt it, but she was holding her breath. She let it out like a small sigh when he thanked her and moved past her, heading toward the bathroom. I'd never seen Sarah like this before.

She busied herself with the movie, and I suggested we order a pizza. She nodded, going to get the number. As I snuggled into one end of the couch—"my" end—I heard her actually humming to herself in the kitchen. David joined her there. I could hear their voices, soft and conversational, and then I heard her low and seductive laugh.

"What do you want on your pizza, Lizzie?" she asked as she pulled David toward the couch. I couldn't take my eyes off their intertwined hands. David sat on the other end of the couch, Sarah between us.

"The usual," I replied coolly. She nodded, pursing her lips for a moment, and then ordered, two larges, just cheese for me on half of one, her usual (and strange) ham and pineapple, and a "loaded" pizza for David. We settled in to watch the movie, and when the pizza came, Sarah and David moved to the floor to eat, but I stayed on the couch, curled into my corner.

I watched them picnicking together, eating out of the box, talking in low voices about Henry Miller—David thought he was adolescent and crude—and, since Anais was cheating on her husband with Henry in the movie, they talked about ex-husbands and ex-wives.

I listened, watching the movie, feeling completely left out and inimitably sad. My half of the pizza finished, I licked my fingers like they were wounds and stretched out on the couch. I had it all to myself now. I watched half-lidded, seeing them having sex in an alley on the screen, her pinned up against the wall, and imagined a cock buried in me like that. Then I didn't know if I was watching or dreaming. The warmth of the fire, my full belly, my eyes closed against the sight of

Sarah and David together, all conspired to slip me toward sleep.

I dozed, in and out, waking slightly when Sarah moved past me, cleaning up pizza boxes. I saw David with his shirt off, wearing only a pair of sweats, and then slipped back toward dreaming. When I woke again, my eyes slowly flickering open, I thought I could still hear the soft cries of Anais in the movie, but when I looked, the screen was a clear blue. The movie had ended. Tilting my head slightly, I saw David and Sarah tangled together on the rug in front of the fire, kissing deeply. I bit my lip to keep from gasping out loud, and let my eyes fall back to slits, not wanting them to know I was awake.

He kissed her mouth, her neck, and she made the soft, familiar cries I knew meant his hand was between her legs. I couldn't see from this angle, his body blocked hers, but her thigh was up over his, and it was bare. Her hand was in that dark curly hair, moving down the strong muscles of his back. He moved on top of her then, still wearing sweats, and I saw she was completely nude. She opened her legs to take his weight, wrapping herself around him, all soft tawny limbs. He nuzzled her breasts, and groaned out loud when she fumbled past the elastic band of his sweats.

"Shh." Sarah glanced toward me on the couch.

I looked at her through my lashes and held perfectly still, breathing deeply, as if still sleeping. She seemed satisfied, and I watched her hand begin to move rhythmically under his sweats as he held himself above her and thrust against her, his arms ropes of muscle in the firelight.

I bit my lip, aching to see what she had in her hand. She moved out from under him, gently pushing on his chest, and he rolled easily to his back. His cock tented the fabric as she teased and rubbed with the flat of her palm. I heard his breathing getting faster and more rough. She eased down between his legs, kneeling there, and

I saw in his eyes how beautiful he thought she was...and she was.

His breath drew in sharply when she touched her own body, running her hands up over her breasts, lifting them, letting them fall. She stroked her belly, pulled at her downy, blonde pubic hair, cupped her pussy with her hand, and then used two fingers to spread it open for him. He nodded, watching her, sucking air through his teeth sharply when she eased his sweats down over his hips to let his cock spring free. I was stunned by the sweet length of it, by the pre-cum I saw glistening on the tip as Sarah rubbed a finger over and then lifted to her mouth to taste.

"I want your mouth," he whispered, glancing at me, and I quickly assumed the through-my-eyelashes vision and deep breathing routine, although it was getting more difficult to breathe normally as I watched them.

Sarah glanced at me, too, then back at him. She smiled and nodded, but didn't take him in her mouth but her hand, rubbing the tip with her palm at first, then grasping it firmly and stroking. His eyes closed as he made a small growl sound at the back of his throat with every stroke. His head started to move from side to side, his breath coming faster, and she slowed, pulling the skin down tight.

"Yes," he whispered when she ran the fingers of her other hand over his balls, cupping them, rubbing them gently. Seeing her do that, watching the hunger in her eyes as she looked at the length of his cock, made my whole body tingle. She leaned over it, blowing on it, kissing the tip gently, and then took the length of it into her mouth. It simply disappeared. His head went back, mouth open, his hips instinctively pushing toward her and his hand going to her head.

I watched her, eager, my eyes wide open now but knowing their focus was fully on each other. I watched her take him into her mouth over and over, his hand buried in her hair. She stopped, licking the tip, licking her lips, and I saw how red and swollen her mouth was from him, like she'd just eaten cherries. I shifted on the couch, and felt my clit throb in response. I wanted to touch it, rub it, but didn't want to call attention to myself.

She eased her way up his body, straddling him, with his cock pulsing against her belly. He reached up to cup her breasts, thumbing the nipples and making her rock gently against him, moaning softly. She moved up onto her knees, reaching down to take him in her hand, rubbing the length of him against her pussy, through her slit.

"It's been quite a while since I've had a cock in me," she whispered, meeting his eyes. His hands were on her hips, rocking her gently.

"Do you want it?" he asked softly.

She nodded, closing her eyes, and then he did something that surprised me and surprised her, too, I think. He shifted his weight, moving her off of him, and repositioned himself in behind her as she was kneeling. He pressed himself against her from behind, running his hands over her body, from her breasts to between her legs, not stopping to concentrate on one thing, simply exploring her quickly but thoroughly with his hands. He pushed her forward onto her hands and knees, and she looked back over her shoulder at him, biting her lip. His cock was standing straight up, pulsing, and the sight of it resting against her ass was thrilling to me.

I struggled to control my breathing as I slid my hand through the slit in the front of the robe, under the elastic of my panties, to find my aching clit as I watched him take his cock into his hand and rub it against her ass. His pre-cum glistened there in the firelight. He grabbed her hips and positioned her. I heard her whimper, but she arched her back, giving him better access. He looked down at her, spreading her cheeks open with his hands, using his fingers to spread her pussy. I couldn't see it, I could only see them from the side, but I knew what he was doing, and saw him looking intensely at her little hole.

"Please," she moaned. "Ohhh, David, please, put it in me."

It seemed to be what he was waiting for. He grabbed his cock and slid it through her and then into her. She shuddered and gasped, moving back to meet him. He grunted, grabbing her hips to steady her, easing slowly back out. I saw her juices slick on him as he did, and it made my mouth water, for her pussy or his cock, I wasn't sure which.

I tried to be quiet, moving just my fingers lightly, almost imperceptibly, over my clit, keeping my breathing deep, but I couldn't seem to help it from becoming faster and harder as I watched him start to fuck her. Sarah mewled, really like a cat, and the familiar sound of it went straight to my core.

He'd started slow, moving easily—I could *hear* how wet she was!—in and out, and she'd moved from her soft sighs to the kitteny kinds of sounds she made, but the intensity was building. He wasn't going easy anymore, he wasn't being gentle, he was really slamming hard into her now, and this started eliciting deeper sounds from her. They had completely forgotten me.

David suddenly grabbed her thigh and somehow maneuvered her so she was rolling over and onto her back, without ever sliding out of her. He pushed his hips hard forward to make sure, balls–deep, and she gasped. I bit my lip to keep from moaning, my fingers moving just a little faster on my clit, making delicious circles there.

His hands, large, strong hands, I noticed, lifted her ass a little, pulling her in closer. She put both legs up, and he leaned into her, letting her legs fall over his shoulders. He was working hard now, and she was taking him, each stroke from tip to base, again and again. I couldn't believe he hadn't come. How could he fuck her like that, so persistently, and not come? My clit throbbed with the urge, and I had to press it hard and wait, my breath lost in the sound of their sex, but he seemed undaunted.

She moaned fully now, eyes closed, lost in sensation. I saw him in the firelight, focusing on her face, watching every movement, seeing and reveling in her pleasure. Something he saw made him shift his weight, not slowing in the least. Her eyes flew open and she clutched at him, her nails digging into his biceps. He held her gaze with his as he moved more deeply into her, and I watched her open, her legs shifting, widening, her whole posture changing, receiving him.

What I saw made my breath change. Something had completely shifted in the room. It was different now, his movements, her response. He was still fucking her, hard, but where she'd been tight, focused, trying to maintain control before, now it was like he was fucking her wide open, more open than I'd ever seen her before.

"Good, yes," he encouraged her lowly, and she moaned.

My fingers moved furiously over my clit, watching and wanting to feel what she was feeling, seeing it in her face, hearing it in the throaty sound of her voice. I'd never seen Sarah like this, so soft and unconcealed, so abandoned. She'd never given herself to me like this. In fact, I'd never seen anyone give themselves over quite like this, and something deep within me ached to surrender to it.

"David...David..." She softly repeated his name, her head moving from side to side, eyes closed, lost in her own pleasure.

"Look at me," he insisted, and I saw her hesitate, perhaps not wanting to pull herself out or give herself over. "Sarah, look in my eyes."

Slowly, she did, and he nodded, their eyes locked. He had nearly stopped now, just barely moving into her. I was three feet away and I felt the energy between them, the deep connection, and I ached for it. God, I wanted him to touch *me*, fuck *me*, look at *me*, look *through* me and *into me*, just that way.

He began moving again, and she met him, with her body, with her eyes. They rocked together, and with every movement I saw her opening more, giving more of herself over to him, matching his movements, his breath. Her hands dug deep into his shoulders, pulling him closer and closer, his weight fully on her now as they moved together, almost like one body, one entity, merged and slick with sweat.

My fingers on my clit matched their intensity, their speed, my eyes full of the sight of them in the firelight even when I closed them. Watching Sarah with a man was beyond my expectations or my fantasies. I'd never imagined her like this, so soft, open, surrendered to both the sensation and to the man inside of her. The difference was startling and exciting to me.

"David, so close," she whispered and I heard him take a deep, sustained breath as she began to buck and moan.

"Come," he said. "Here. Right here...into my eyes...into my mouth."

He held her chin with one hand, finding her mouth with his, looking into her eyes as she came. Her familiar intake of and held breath, following by her shuddering sighs were missing. Her sound, muffled against his mouth, was low and seemed to spread out, like waves or ripples on water, until I could feel it tingling through my whole body as I listened to her orgasm.

I expected him to speed up, to push hard into her and come, too, but he didn't. His breath was slow and even, barely moving on her now, riding the waves of her orgasm. Her eyes finally fluttered closed and she turned her face toward me, flushed and open-mouthed. He placed a hand on the center of her chest and she gasped and nearly sobbed, eyes opening in surprise.

And she was looking right into my bewildered and captivated eyes.

Then David turned to look at me, and the intensity and knowing in his gaze left me without breath or words. There was nothing to say, but with both of them focused now fully on me, I felt myself flushing and swallowing hard. Sarah reached her hand out to me, opening and closing her fist like a child asking for a piece of candy. David pressed her arm to her side, kneeling up between her legs. I saw his erection, wet with her juices, still hard, waning only slightly as it pulsed against the apex of her thighs.

I felt paralyzed and full of a deep longing I didn't understand. David seemed to know this, and he moved toward me. My robe was quickly opened and, as his eyes swept my body, I felt my throat constrict, watching his glistening cock grow fatter and more present at the sight of me. He tugged at my panties, and they disappeared over the swell of my thighs, sticking a little at the knees. Then he gathered me up like a little bit of fluff, leaving my robe on the couch, and laid me next to Sarah on the rug.

For a moment I was sure he didn't know what to do with the both of us naked there in front of him. His eyes weren't sure where to travel, distracted by the rise and fall of her breasts, by the wetness spreading to my thighs, until his eyes found hers and she slowly smiled at him. She was lightly stroking the top of my thigh, her hand warm and soft. Then his eyes found mine and I thought I would drown or be consumed by my own hunger, my ache and longing to be his. The world was spinning lazy circles around me and all I knew was David.

Everything he did, every movement he made, seemed full of purpose and intent. I gasped as his hands pressed my thighs open, his eyes never leaving mine. I thought he was just going to enter me immediately and I was braced for it, barely breathing, eyes wide, but his large, rough hands kneaded my flesh, digging deeply into my thighs, and I found myself opening wider, my thighs parting and parting like I couldn't open enough. Sarah stroked my arm, my side, the underside of my breast, her tenderness a direct contrast to his force, her coaxing me at the same time as he was easing me more and more toward an edge of wildness where I found myself afraid to open my eyes.

But David made me open them, keep them open and focused on him, on his eyes, seeking to take me somewhere I'd never been, somewhere I ached to go, a place I was desperate for and at the same time terrified of. And when I looked over at Sarah, pleading with my eyes, I saw she knew, she understood, and I felt the shift in her, knowing suddenly she was allowing all of this because she wanted it for me, but more—it wasn't in her control anymore.

It was then that the trembling started, and I wanted to crawl away, hide. I felt too raw and bare, vulnerable and exposed before them both. And I don't know how he knew what to do, but David took my hands and raised them above my head and pressed his body weight against me, not completely, but enough, holding both of my wrists in his one hand, and he kissed me. It was like falling, like disappearing, like I'd found the edge of that precipice and leaped, or been pushed, and there was nowhere else to go but the bottomless depth that his mouth, the weight of him, the thick hardness resting against my thigh, all pressed me towards.

Suddenly all appetite, I was eager and moaning, sucking at his tongue, my shaking thighs clasped around him as if I could force him to enter me, take me. I felt him smile against my mouth, and he nuzzled my jaw, my neck, whispering something I couldn't hear, but I felt it all through my body, almost a chant, murmured over and over. I felt my body respond, buzzing still but less frantic for him, now more of a yearning breathing me wide open. He whispered, "Good," against my ear and I thought the heat of that praise would melt me into a small puddle on the rug.

I relaxed into his exploration of my body, the murmur of his mouth against my skin, the delicious heat spreading thick like honey or syrup everywhere he touched me. I found myself calling for him, as I'd heard Sarah do, "David, David," my head moving side to side, eyes closed and lost in the sensation.

Then he was above me again, urging me to open my eyes, to see him, and my breath went away the moment I did. I felt more naked than I'd ever been before and closed my eyes again. He kissed my eyelids and whispered, "Elizabeth," my full name, "open your eyes," and it wasn't a request. I couldn't deny him. I whimpered, and he let more of him press into me, the weight of him, his chest, his belly. I felt his cock resting against my wetness and moaned.

And we were there, I don't know how long, his breath matching mine. He was somehow breathing me, entering me with his breath, with his eyes, and I felt something within me break open, dissolve. It was only then that he pushed into me, the size and feel of him a force beyond any physical sensation I'd ever known. This wasn't sex—this wasn't anything like I'd experienced, the urgent, quick fumblings in the backseat or the groping and poking in the basement with Tim—this was like fucking the universe, being fucked by the entire cosmos. There was no me and no him, and it was all me and all him and I knew nothing else.

His rhythm was slow at first, and I squeezed myself around him, wanting more, more, *more*. His movements were controlled but responsive, feeding me a little at a time, as if I were a baby bird, just one enormous, eager hunger. I thought fleetingly of Sarah's poem, and finally understood.

I wiggled and moaned, reaching up for him and wrapping my arms around his shoulders, his neck, my fingers slipping through his curls, and he let me pull him close, closer, and then...then pushed even further into me. Oh God, I didn't realize he'd been holding back the length of him until he fully entered me and the sound that came out of my throat was from some other girl, someone I didn't know, a raw and low and aching sound.

And then he teased me again, only giving me part of him, slow, shallow thrusts, making me pant and squirm and beg beneath him, until finally he moved deeper, harder into me, his arms gathering me toward him, pressing me against his chest, his face buried in my hair. I heard myself moaning from far away, and felt a jolt, like a current, go through me when he would, every now and then, make a small grunting noise and stop for a moment, poised just at the entrance of me, breathing hard. If I wiggled then or pressed upward, his mouth would set in a thin line, his eyes would roll back under their lids, and his breath would simply disappear. And then he'd start again, all deep, even strokes, urging me higher, my whole body buzzing and alive.

I realized I was waiting for him, testing him, teasing him, squeezing him. Tim couldn't last longer than five minutes tops—he always seemed lost the minute he slid into the smooth slickness of me. I didn't expect things to last, considering how long David had been with Sarah. And somehow I think he knew it.

He had that small smile as he fucked me—God how he fucked me!—watching me through those half-lidded, dark eyes. It was like *he* was waiting, and I think he was. Waiting for me to give up, to give in, to find the rhythm and rock with him, and finally, I did. I lost myself completely, and yet I was always aware of how he was filling me, moving me, pushing me.

And then he found just the right spot, moving his cock down and into me, nudging against my clit, again and again and again, but it was when his mouth found my nipples, already painfully pursed and hard, that I felt the last bits of me go. He became hungry, greedy for them, pressing my breasts together and licking them both like tiny cherries. Just watching his tongue lapping, feeling the tickle between my legs growing, flushing my whole body with feeling, pushed me over. I called his name and he looked up at me, nodding, not stopping his motion or his licking, in fact moving just a little more, just a little faster, a little harder, a little deeper, and I found it, the unending place I'd been searching for in his eyes, and I went.

He gave me that orgasm, gave it to me like a gift, and it went on and on, like I was breaking against a shoreline again and again. It crashed and rippled and swirled through me until I shook with the force of it. And I never lost sight of him, the man inside of me, aware of every movement, every feeling, like there was no longer any boundary between us—we were truly one thing.

He watched me, my breath slowing, as he settled himself beside me on an elbow, the coolness of the air on my sweat-beaded skin like a thousand icy kisses. I was floating, still filled with the warmth of his soft praise and his steady hands. It was then I became aware of Sarah, oh my Sarah, watching us, watching me, like she was seeing a flower open for the first time in her life. I wondered if that had been the look on my face when her eyelids had fluttered open to find me watching her with David, that hungry, awed, rapture of attention. I thought it probably was.

I reached my arm out for her and she snuggled into my other side. I looked back and forth between them with nothing short of wonder and awe. I didn't realize until later, it was sort of like being a child in my parent's bed when I was very, very little.

They were both looking at me with such soft, open tenderness and love. I felt completely filled. Then Sarah's eyes shifted to David, and I saw it again, some longing or ache for him I couldn't share, and when I looked to him, I found it there, too, and felt it more keenly, my jealousy, like a thing outside of me creeping in.

I swallowed it down. I tried hard, feeling suddenly cold. Sarah reached over my body and I thought she was going to hold me, but her hand found his cock. Oh my God, I felt it. He was still hard and she smiled as she touched him, stroking him against my thigh. His breath came a little faster, his eyes fluttering closed for a moment, and I watched her watching him, saw the yearning in her eyes, felt her breath matching his, and felt my own building to match theirs.

Sarah didn't stop touching him, but she leaned down and kissed me. The softness of her, the yielding ripeness of her mouth, was so different and exciting to me. I moaned as she kissed my nipples, soft, feathery kisses, and my body responded instantly, feeling her hair brush over my chest and my belly. I looked down at her hand on his cock and wanted it, too.

I reached for him, covering her hand with mine and she smiled at me and then up at him. His eyes registered his delight, his anticipation, seeing both of our hands entwined, moving together along the shaft. Sarah moved to the other side of him, so now he was between us. She edged down his body to lick the tip of his cock, and I felt her tongue move over my fingers. She kissed and licked him, just over the head, as our hands moved faster. I couldn't resist touching my tongue to his small, soft brown nipple, and moaned when I felt it harden.

David's hand reached out to Sarah, pulling her hips toward him, so she was kneeling up, her mouth still licking at his cock, but he could reach her wetness now, and he wanted it. I watched his fingers probe her open, rubbing along the soft blonde hair, slipping inside of her. The deeper his fingers went, the further she swallowed him until our hands were just encircling the base, keeping his cock steady.

I wanted his fingers, too, and maneuvered myself so I was in the same position as Sarah on the other side of him, arching my back, spreading my thighs a little, offering myself to him. Sarah's mouth moved over his cock, kissing and nibbling, and as my eyes met hers, I leaned in to kiss her over the tip of him. He moaned at the sensation of both of our mouths moving, our tongues finding each other, and that's when his fingers found me, too, easing through the wetness he'd created, probing the deepest parts of me. I gasped and wiggled, pushing back against him.

I don't know how long we took turns taking the length of him while he held each of us in his hands. I liked sliding my tongue down to suck his balls, feeling the weight of them, drawing the loose, soft fuzzy skin into my mouth. We drove him to distraction, I could tell by the way his fingers lost focus inside of me and became driven, mindless pounding against my flesh. It made me even wetter—I felt it seeping down my thighs. Sarah moaned around his cock, and I could tell she was very close to coming from his fingers. She let her flushed cheek rest against his thigh as he took her there, and I took the opportunity to take him fully into my mouth.

Watching her orgasm was so sweet, and I felt his fingers just toying with me while he concentrated on her. I put my energy into sucking him, tasting him, feeling him pulse and swell in my mouth. He moaned and thrust, spurred on by her orgasm. I felt his balls tightening under my fingers. I ached to feel him flood over my tongue and worked harder.

He grunted, shifting his weight a little. He was struggling, working not to come, I could feel it. Sarah's hand was on mine then, massaging his balls. She moved between his legs, stretching herself out between them, and her tongue meshed with mine around his cock. I mirrored her position, stretched out against his other leg, squeezed in against her softness, and he sat up on his elbows, looking down at us.

I could imagine what we looked like. I'd seen us in mirrors, our energy together, dancing at the club, and watched us naked in the mirror over Sarah's bed, a vision, and now our mouths red and swollen from sucking him, our pussies wet and satisfied but our eyes still hungry for him, blonde and red hair mingling as we gently fought over his cock. He watched for a moment, bemused, then moved so he was leaning back against the couch, his hands finding our hair, moving our heads. I gasped out loud when he pulled me back by my hair—it wasn't hard, but hard enough—and aimed his cock into Sarah's mouth.

She swallowed him eagerly, expertly, and he moved his fingers then over my cheek, to my lips, rubbing them, letting me lick his fingers, suck them. That sensation alone made him moan out loud, and his eyes rolled back slightly, his body shaking a little. He grabbed Sarah's hair then, pulling her back like he'd pulled me, and pressed me toward him. I was less sure, but hungry, and sucked him hard, liking the feeling of him moving in my mouth, the warm flood of pre-cum now and then spurring me on.

"Ah Lizzie," he moaned, pulling out of my mouth, and the sound of my name, the sound of his voice, made me flush. "Girl, you're too much."

My whole body smiled. If I'd been a dog tail, I would have been furiously wagging. He touched my lips, tenderly, my cheeks, my eyelids, my hair. "I'm going to fuck Sarah," he told me, I think by way of explanation. I nodded, acquiescing, moving aside, and somehow Sarah just knew what he wanted, and moved to her hands and knees, hugging a large pillow from the couch beneath her.

"Lizzie, get the K-Y from the drawer," she murmured. I reached over to the end table and pulled it out. I'd always teased her about it—it seemed too naughty, having it anywhere but the bathroom or the bedroom—but she insisted on having it everywhere we might use it, and that included there in front of the fireplace.

David kneeled up and offered the length of himself to me. I kissed and nibbled at him first, flicking open the tube and warming some in my hands. Then I slid my hands over him, up and down. He swallowed hard, his eyes closing again. Then he took aim, and my mouth opened slightly, incredulous, as he slid the tip upward from the pink wetness of her pussy toward the small, puckered hole above. I felt my whole body tense and go cold.

Sarah waited, her thighs trembling slightly, and she gasped as he started, easing his weight slowly, slowly forward, pressing into her. Her hands curled into fists on the pillow beneath her, and she bit her lip. At first I was concerned, appalled, aghast, watching him push inch by inch into a place so dark, so secret...I couldn't even have imagined this happening. But Sarah moaned, winced, moaned again, whispered, "Yes, more," and he listened to her, placed his hand underneath her belly and stilled her, until finally he was completely buried inside of her.

"David, God, yes," she moaned, looking back at him. "Fuck my ass."

The words thrilled me, and so did the guttural cry she gave when he began to move. My still K-Y wet hands moved immediately between my own legs as I knelt, watching. David glanced at me, his eyes drinking me in. Then he was focused again on Sarah, his movements slow and shallow at first, like he had been inside of me, then deeper, harder, as she moaned and bucked, urging him on.

His hands moved to her hips, taking her, pushing her, and she gasped, groaned, begged, please, please, his name rolling off her tongue over and over like water. I saw her slide her fingers into her pussy as he fucked her. My own fingers on my clit worked furiously, unable to believe the stretch of her, taking him, again and again, imagining what it must feel like to be so wide open in such a vulnerable place. And then Sarah was coming, rubbing herself and coming hard. I saw her muscles squeezing, squeezing him.

David moaned, and somehow crossed a line, calling her name. He slid his cock almost all the way out of her, letting that ring of flesh rub just against the tip of him, in and out, and then he was coming, too. I watched him flood out of her, the sticky white stuff sliding slowly down her slit toward where her fingers were pressed to her clit. The sight of his cum, seeing his head thrown back, watching his cock pulse and twitch, sent me over my own edge, and

I let my orgasm ease its way through me slowly, throbbing, trembling, until I collapsed on the rug next to Sarah, moving in to share her pillow.

She smiled, looking at me through half-closed eyes. "Was it worth it?" she whispered hoarsely. I looked up at David, still holding her hips and looking down at both of us. His eyes were on her, like he could swallow her whole. I had a feeling this was going to cost me a great deal, but I just whispered, "yes," and kissed her cheek.

David made his way down to the pillow between us, pulling us both in, and we fit perfectly against his chest. I think we dozed, on and off, but we made love for hours again that night, she and he and I, in so many ways and so many positions I forgot where any of us began or ended.

And we were together a few more times that summer, but something was growing large between David and Sarah, and edging me further out. When I left for college that year, my goodbye to Sarah was bittersweet.

She was nonchalant about it, but I like to think now it was just a defense, that she didn't really want to let me go. My goodbye to David was harder, somehow. He held me and rocked me and I knew he knew, how much I loved them both, how much I wanted, how impossible it all was.

I never saw her again, after all that. We said we'd keep in touch, but life happened. And, as Sarah once said, it pretty much sucked. And it kept on sucking. Tim and I broke up, and I found a new boyfriend, someone older, more experienced. Then Sarah moved out of state. She gave me a forwarding address, but I couldn't find the words to write. It just wasn't the same. I didn't know if David went with her, or perhaps... she went with David.

Until one afternoon a few years ago, I saw David in Logan airport being frisked by TSA with a toddler in tow. The little girl was blonde, blue-eyed, the sweetest baby I'd ever seen, even with a ring of chocolate around her perfect, pink rosebud mouth.

She looked just like her mother, and I knew, even before David saw me, met my eyes, smiled and waved.

They had found their happy ending.

The End

GET SIX FREE READS!
Selena loves hearing from readers!
website: selenakitt.com
facebook: facebook.com/selenakittfanpage
twitter: twitter.com/selenakitt @selenakitt
blog: http://selenakitt.com/blog

Get ALL SIX of Selena Kitt's FREE READS
by joining her mailing list!

ABOUT SELENA KITT

Selena Kitt is a NEW YORK TIMES bestselling and award-winning author of erotic and romance fiction. She is one of the highest selling erotic writers in the business with over two million books sold!

Her writing embodies everything from the spicy to the scandalous, but watch out- this kitty also has sharp claws and her stories often include intriguing edges and twists that take readers to new, thought-provoking depths.

When she's not pawing away at her keyboard, Selena runs an innovative publishing company (excessica.com) and bookstore (excitica.com), as well as two erotica and erotic romance promotion companies (excitesteam.com and excitespice.com) and she now runs the Erotica Readers and Writers Association.

Her books EcoErotica (2009), The Real Mother Goose (2010) and Heidi and the Kaiser (2011) were all Epic Award Finalists. Her only gay male romance, Second Chance, won the Epic Award in Erotica in 2011. Her story, Connections, was one of the runners-up for the 2006 Rauxa Prize, given annually to an erotic short story of "exceptional literary quality."

Her book, Babysitting the Baumgartners, is now an adult film by Adam & Eve, starring Mick Blue, Anikka Albrite, Sara Luvv and A.J. Applegate.

She can be reached on her website at:
www.selenakitt.com

Did You Know?

BABYSITTING THE BAUMGARTNERS

Is Now a Motion Picture from Adam & Eve?

Starring

Anikka Albrite

Mick Blue

Sara Luvv

A.J. Applegate

Directed by Kay Brandt

EXCERPT from
BABYSITTING THE BAUMGARTNERS:

When my legs felt steady enough to hold me, I got out of the shower and dried off, wrapping myself in one of the big white bath sheets. My room was across the hall from the bathroom, and the Baumgartner's was the next room over. The kids' rooms were at the other end of the hallway.

As I made my way across the hall, I heard Mrs. B's voice from behind their door. "You want that tight little nineteen-year-old pussy, Doc?"

I stopped, my heart leaping, my breath caught. *Oh my God.* Were they talking about me? He said something, but it was low, and I couldn't quite make it out. Then she said, "Just wait until I wax it for you. It'll be soft and smooth as a baby."

Shocked, I reached down between my legs, cupping my pussy as if to protect it, standing there transfixed, listening. I stepped closer to their door, seeing it wasn't completely closed, still trying to hear what they were saying. There wasn't any noise, now.

"Oh God!" I heard him groan. "Suck it harder."

My eyes wide, I felt the pulse returning between my thighs, a slow, steady heat. Was she sucking his cock? I remembered what it looked like in his hand--even from a distance, I could tell it was big--much bigger than any of the boys I'd ever been with.

"Ahhhh fuck, Carrie!" He moaned. I bit my lip, hearing Mrs. B's first name felt so wrong, somehow. "Take it all, baby!"

All?! My jaw dropped as I tried to imagine, pressing my hand over my throbbing mound. Mrs. B said something, but I couldn't hear it, and as I leaned toward the door, I bumped it with the towel wrapped around my hair. My hand went to my mouth and I took an involuntary step back as the door edged open just a crack. I turned to go to my room, but I knew that they would hear the sound of my door.

"You want to fuck me, baby?" she purred. "God, I'm so wet ... did you see her sweet little tits?"

"Fuck, yeah," he murmured. "I wanted to come all over them."

Hearing his voice, I stepped back toward the door, peering through the crack. The bed was behind the door, at the opposite angle, but there was a large vanity table and mirror against the other wall, and I could see them reflected in it. Mrs. B was completely naked, kneeling over him. I saw her face, her breasts swinging as she took him into her mouth. His cock stood straight up in the air.

"She's got beautiful tits, doesn't she?" Mrs. B ran her tongue up and down the shaft.

"Yeah." His hand moved in her hair, pressing her down onto his cock. "I want to see her little pussy so bad. God, she's so beautiful."

"Do you want to see me eat it?" She moved up onto him, still stroking his cock. "Do you want to watch me lick that sweet, shaved cunt?"

I pressed a cool palm to my flushed cheek, but my other hand rubbed the towel between my legs as I watched. I'd never heard anyone say that word out loud and it both shocked and excited me.

"Oh God, yeah!" He grabbed her tits as they swayed over him. I saw her riding him, and knew he must be inside of her. "I want inside her tight little cunt."

I moved the towel aside and slipped my fingers between my lips.

He's talking about me!

The thought made my whole body tingle, and my pussy felt on fire. Already slick and wet from my orgasm in the shower, my fingers slid easily through my slit.

"I want to fuck her while she eats your pussy." He thrust up into her, his hands gripping her hips. Her breasts swayed as they rocked together. My eyes widened at the image he conjured, but Mrs. B moaned, moving faster on top of him.

"Yeah, baby!" She leaned over, her breasts dangling in his face. His hands went to them, his mouth sucking at her nipples, making her squeal and slam down against him even harder. "You want her on her hands and knees, her tight little ass in the air?"

He groaned, and I rubbed my clit even faster as he grabbed her and practically threw her off him onto the bed. She seemed to know what he wanted, because she got onto her hands and knees and he fucked her like that, from behind. The sound of them, flesh slapping against flesh, filled the room.

They were turned toward the mirror, but Mrs. B had her face buried in her arms, her ass lifted high in the air. Doc's eyes looked down between their legs, like he was watching himself slide in and out of her.

"Fuck!" Mrs. B's voice was muffled. "Oh fuck, Doc! Make me come!"

He grunted and drove into her harder. I watched her shudder and grab the covers in her fists. He didn't stop, though--his hands grabbed her hips and he worked himself into her over and over. I felt weak-kneed and full of heat, my fingers rubbing my aching clit in fast little circles. Mrs. B's orgasm had almost sent me right over the edge. I was very, very close.

"That tight nineteen-year-old cunt!" He shoved into her. "I want to taste her." He slammed into her again. "Fuck her." And again. "Make her come." And again. "Make her scream until she can't take anymore."

I leaned my forehead against the doorjamb for support, trying to control how fast my breath was coming, how fast my climax was coming, but I couldn't. I whimpered, watching him fuck her and knowing he was imagining me ... *me!*

"Come here." He pulled out and Mrs. B turned around like she knew what he wanted. "Swallow it."

He knelt up on the bed as she pumped and sucked at his cock. I saw the first spurt land against her cheek, a thick white strand of cum, and then she covered the head with her mouth and swallowed, making soft mewing noises in her throat. I came then, too, shuddering and shivering against the doorframe, biting my lip to keep from crying out.

When I opened my eyes and came to my senses, Mrs. B was still on her hands and knees, focused between his legs--but Doc was looking right at me, his dark eyes on mine.

He saw me. For the second time today-- he saw me.

My hand flew to my mouth and I stumbled back, fumbling for the doorknob behind me I knew was there. I finally found it, slipping into my room and shutting the door behind me. I leaned against it, my heart pounding, my pussy dripping, and wondered what I was going to do now.

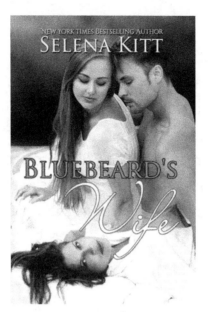

BLUEBEARD'S WIFE

What would you do, if you found out your husband was secretly calling in to phone sex lines? Confront him? Throw him out? Divorce him?

Nope! Instead of getting angry, curious Tara decides to start listening in on John's steamy conversations. She can't help herself, because her laconic husband has never shared a fantasy with his wife during their entire marriage. But it turns out he's been leading a double life, telling other women what he really wants in the bedroom!

When a frustrated Tara turns to her best friend, Kelly, for advice, her much more adventurous partner-in-crime hatches a plan to bring John and Tara together. Once the trap is set, using Kelly as bait, the two women spring it on one unsuspecting man whose fantasies are about to become a very sexy reality.

EXCERPT from <u>BLUEBEARD'S WIFE</u>:

"Tara, do you know what I wanted to do to you when you came downstairs in that dress?"

I shook my head, turning a little toward him.

John reached a hand out and fingered the soft, satin hem that was riding high on my thighs. "I wanted to tear it off you."

"You did?" I asked, my eyes wide. He was looking down at where my dress ended.

"I wanted to tear it off you and take you, right there, up against the wall in the hallway." His voice was hoarse, and I swallowed hard.

"You did?" I squeaked.

"Seeing you dancing out there with Kelly—you don't know how sexy you are, do you?" he asked, leaning over to me, his hand running up from my knee to my thigh. His breath was warm on my face, and I could smell the 7&7's he'd been drinking all night. My own head was still swimming with wine.

"You two rubbing up against each other, seeing your red little dress riding up and up," he whispered, his hand pushing my dress up further as he sought higher ground on my leg. "You looked just like you do when you come, with your eyes half closed and your mouth open and your legs quivering."

I moaned, tilting my face up to him, and then he was kissing me, his tongue forcing its way past my teeth, down my throat, as he pressed me into the door. "I wanted to fuck you right there on the dance floor," he growled against my neck, biting and sucking at my flesh. "I wanted to fuck you both."

I gasped, his hands groping me in the dark, everywhere at once. My dress was pushed up to my waist now, his fingers rubbing fast and hard between my legs. We kissed, our mouths meshing together as he leaned over the gearshift to get to me. When he pulled my panties aside and plunged his fingers into me, I hissed, putting one foot up onto the dashboard to give him better access.

He was trying to climb over onto me but there wasn't enough room—not in his little Roadster. When I whispered that fact to him, he grunted, pulling his hand away from me and moving to open his door. A moment later, he was opening mine, and I was still sitting there with my panties askew, my heels off, and my dress shoved up to my waist, struggling with the seatbelt.

YOU'VE REACHED

"THE END!"

BUY THIS AND MORE TITLES AT
www.eXcessica.com

EROTICA FLAVORS FOR ALL
Facebook Group
facebook.com/groups/eroticaflavors

Check us out for updates
about eXcessica books!

CPSIA information can be obtained
at www.ICGtesting.com
Printed in the USA
LVHW082335060619
620472LV00031B/773/P